"Don't call me that," Karen muttered

She was angry at her own feelings as she said, "I'm not your love."

"I'll be the judge of that," Val retorted, stepping toward her. He raised a hand and touched her hair. "It's still a beautiful color." His dark eyes warmed with a smile. "You've worn well over the years, sweetheart. I'm glad you've come."

"I only came to take Tony home," she said flatly, "I'm not staying."

"Of course you are," he replied. "We'll have a few days here together, the three of us, so that we can come to a permanent arrangement for living together."

"I'm not going to marry you," she replied tautly. "I'm going to marry Paul Dutton."

"Not if I can prevent it," Val argued, his eyes losing their warmth. "I'm not having my son brought up by a stranger."

FLORA KIDD

between pride and passion

Harlequin Books

TORONTO • NEW YORK • LOS ANGELES • LONDON
AMSTERDAM • PARIS • SYDNEY • HAMBURG
STOCKHOLM • ATHENS • TOKYO • MILAN

Harlequin Presents first edition December 1982
ISBN 0-373-10554-1

Original hardcover edition published in 1982
by Mills & Boon Limited

Printed in U.S.A.

CHAPTER ONE

THE Friday afternoon traffic was heavy and the three lanes of the highway were jammed with cars, trucks and trailers all streaming westwards into shafts of bright sunlight which forced many drivers to slow down cautiously because they were unable to see beyond the dazzle of yellow light, even if they were wearing sunglasses.

It was hot, too, for the middle weekend of October, and Karen Carne rolled down the window of her small car as she waited for the traffic lights at an intersection to change. Immediately she regretted having opened the window as she was almost choked by the fumes from the diesel truck which was in the next lane and just ahead of her.

At last the green filter light began to flicker. The car in front leapt forward and with a screech of tyres swung to the left. Changing gear rapidly, Karen followed it across the rows of cars which were waiting to surge forward along the highway towards the city. A quick right and then another left turn and she reached a wide tree-lined avenue which was the main road of the suburb where she lived.

She glanced at her watch. Twenty past three. School would be out. She hoped Tony, her six-year-old son, had remembered she would be picking him up to go shopping for clothes at a sale of children's winter parkas and boots at one of the departmental stores in the shopping mall.

The school building, single-storeyed, flat-roofed, grey-walled, with green and white trim around its wide windows, loomed up on the right and she stopped the car by the kerb. There were still a few chilren about. Some were loitering along the avenue under the shade of tall drooping elms, kicking at the crisp yellow leaves which lay in heaps on the widewalk. Some were playing ball in the school yard. As far as she could see Tony wasn't one of the boys playing ball, nor was he waiting on the shallow flight of steps which led up to the main entrance of the building, so she assumed he was inside.

Her slim figure set off by the narrow skirt and fitted jacket of her suit of yellow and brown tweed, her long shapely legs flattered by the high-heeled sandals she was wearing, her thick wavy copper-coloured hair glinting with golden highlights in the bright sunlight as she moved, Karen pulled open one of the double doors and entered the wide hallway. The place was empty and silent. Tony wasn't waiting for her there.

From a room on the right came the tapping sound of a typewriter. Heels clicking on the oak blocks of the floor, she went towards the room. On the blue door was the word OFFICE in white letters. The door was slightly open and as she drummed with her knuckles on the panel Karen pushed the door open further. A grey-haired woman wearing a green pants suit and a white blouse was sitting behind a desk typing busily. On the desk was a wooden sign announcing that she was Phyllis Craig, School Secretary.

'Excuse me,' said Karen. 'I'm Tony Carne's mother. I told him to wait at school until I came for him this afternoon. Do you know if he's still here?'

'Whose class is he in?' snapped Phyllis Craig. Her large face was pale and her eyes looked tired. She looked as if she had had enough of school for one week and could hardly wait to leave it.

'Miss Watson's,' replied Karen.

'Ah, yes, I remember.' Mrs Craig's face softened slightly and she picked up a notebook to flick the pages over. 'Mr Mackindall left a message for you. Tony's father came to the school at lunch time and asked permission to take Tony out for his meal. Mr Mackindall agreed to let the boy go, but Tony didn't come back for afternoon school.'

'Tony's father?' echoed Karen incredulously. She had the strangest feeling that cold hard fingers had curled about her heart and were squeezing it, cutting off the blood supply to her brain and her limbs. She swayed slightly and then sat down abruptly on the nearest chair. Her dark brown eyes wide and staring, she leaned forward. 'Did you see him? The man who said he was Tony's father, I mean,' she said hoarsely.

'Of course I did,' replied Mrs Craig with a touch of impatience. She was taking a phial from her handbag which lay on the desk and was shaking two white pills into the palm of her hand. She tossed the pills into her mouth, picked up a glass half full of water and drank. 'Excuse me,' she said.

'I've the worst headache. Today has been hectic and I've a pile of letters to finish before I can leave. You were saying?'

'I asked you if you'd seen the man who said he was Tony's father,' Karen repeated.

'I did. Everyone who comes to the school comes to this office first,' said Mrs Craig with a sigh.

'What did he look like?'

'Really, Mrs Carne. I haven't time for this sort of thing. Surely you know what your own husband looks like?'

'I don't have a husband,' retorted Karen coldly. 'And I am not Mrs Carne. Mrs Carne is my mother. Tony's father and I are not married.' She watched the woman's pale face register shock. 'Mr Mackindall knows that. Is he here still?' She glanced towards another blue door which communicated with the office of the school principal.

'No. He left early too. That's why he left a messsge for you with me.'

'And you don't remember what the man who said he was Tony's father looked like,' said Karen, softly accusing. 'I wish you would try to remember. You see, it's most important that I know Tony is with his father and hasn't gone off with a complete stranger.'

Mrs Craig's grey eyes grew round. Her broad-lipped mouth fell open.

'My God!' she gasped. 'You think that. . . .' She stopped, shaking her head from side to side. 'Oh, no! Mr Mackindall wouldn't let *anyone* take a child away from the school. He would make sure the man was Tony's father all right,' she added.

'Was he tall?' demanded Karen sharply. 'Taller than I am?' She rose to her feet.

'Yes, yes, he was. An inch or two over six feet, I'd say.'

'And did he have black hair, longish and untidy?'

'Mmm. It was black, but not too untidy, curved over his shirt collar at the back. And I remember noticing now that he was very tanned, as if he'd been working in the sun a lot. The tan made his eyes look very light. . . .'

'He was Val,' murmured Karen, not sure whether she should feel relieved or even more anxious to know that Tony was with Valentine Knight. 'Tony's father,' she explained quickly in answer to Mrs Craig's enquiring look. 'I expect you're thinking I'm crazy,' she rushed on. 'And I'm sorry to have bothered you. You see, I wasn't expecting him to come today . . . Tony's father . . . and—well, you hear such stories these days about children being snatched by strangers and sometimes held to ransom or . . . or . . . even murdered.' She shivered slightly.

'That's all right. I understand now,' said Mrs Craig comfortingly. She smiled. It was obviously an effort for her, but she did smile. 'I expect you'll find them both at home waiting for you when you get there.'

'I hope so,' said Karen. 'Thank you. Good afternoon, and have a good weekend.'

Karen couldn't get away from the school quickly enough. She ran from the yard to the car. Inside the car was hot and stuffy and she let down the window again. The steering wheel seemed to sear her hands as she turned it and drove down the avenue to turn right at the end on to the winding road beside the glittering lake.

Her heart was knocking against her ribs and her throat felt dry. Val had picked Tony up from school, she had no doubts about that now. The man described by Mrs Craig couldn't be anyone else but Val. Why had he come? What did he want? He should have let her know he was coming. He should have told her he wanted to see Tony. How had he known which school to go to? There was only one answer to that: he must have called at the house first and her mother had told him.

She turned into the avenue where she lived. The leaves of maples glowed orange-red in the sunlight, purple in the shade. Silver trunks of birches glinted against blue-green spruces, lawns were smooth and green, flower beds blazed with October colours—orange, scarlet, crimson and bronze. Neat behind their lawns and trees houses shimmered white, each one a different design yet each one seeming the same as the next; clean, tidy boxes with bland shining windows, coloured front doors and double garages.

There was a car in the driveway at seventeen-twenty, the split-level where Karen lived with her mother, Pamela Carne, and the sight of it gave her hope; the hope that Val had brought Tony home. As she turned into the driveway and parked behind it, she realised it was a car she knew only too well. It belonged to her elder sister Iris, and Babs and Tina, Iris's two daughters, were on the lawn of the house next door, playing with the two girls who lived there. Tony was not with them.

'Mother? Iris? Where are you?' she called as she stepped into the hallway.

'On the sun-deck,' Iris called back.

Where else would either of them be on such a day but on the deck at the back of the house, exercising their housewifely prerogatives to do nothing all afternoon if they felt like doing nothing; to lounge in the sun, soaking up its heat and sipping long cold drinks from tall frosted glasses, not caring in the least that her child had not yet arrived home from school.

'Mother, has Val been here?' Karen demanded as soon as she stepped out on to the deck through the sliding patio window of the family room.

Pamela Carne turned her head, her fair greying hair shimmering in the sunlight. Although over fifty, she didn't look her age, having kept her figure. She was wearing a green and white summer dress which revealed her tanned throat and arms. Tinted glasses shaded her eyes.

'Val who?' she queried vaguely.

'Val-Valentine Knight, of course,' snapped Karen irritably, slipping off her jacket and hanging it over the back of the chair on which she sat down. She was overdressed for the heat of the afternoon, but that morning when she had left home the air had been frostily crisp. Now her hose were sticking to her legs and feet. Slowly she eased her sandals off. As soon as she had found out if Val had been here she would go upstairs to shower and change.

'Is he in town?' asked Iris, lunging up from the

lounger on which she had been lying full length. Her dark brown hair clung in tiny curls to her well-shaped head, framing her pretty oval face. She was also wearing a summer dress—an old one, a shabby cotton thing of pale pink. Her brown eyes, a slightly darker shade than Karen's, glinted with interest. 'Will I get to meet him at last?' she added.

'I don't know. That's why I'm asking Mother if he's been here this afternoon,' replied Karen. That feeling of fingers squeezing her heart was back; it was a feeling of fear. 'Has he been here, Mother?' she asked again.

'No.' Pamela was looking much more alert now. 'At least, not as far as I know. I was out shopping for a couple of hours. I got back just after three, then Iris arrived. Where's Tony? I thought you were going to take him to Bruton's sale?'

'I was.' God, why was it difficult suddenly to speak? Not only was her circulation being cut off but she was also having difficulty breathing and her lips were quivering so much they were having a hard time shaping the words properly. 'But he wasn't at school when I arrived there. Mrs Craig, the secretary, said that Mr Mackindall ... he's the principal ... had let Tony leave at lunch time with ... with ... his father.' Her voice faltered on the last word and died. She cleared her throat. 'So I supposed Val must have called here first and you'd told him which school to go to,' she added.

They both stared at her in silence, then Iris said quietly,

'Are you sure it was Val who picked Tony up?'

'As sure as I can be. I managed to get a sort of description of the man out of Mrs Craig and it sounded like Val. She said also that Mr Mackindall wouldn't let any child leave school with just anyone who came.'

'But how could Mr Mackindall be sure that the man who came for Tony is Tony's father?' retorted Iris argumentatively. 'You've never admitted to anyone in authority that the kid has a father. You've taken a great deal of pride in being a single parent ever since you knew you were pregnant. You wouldn't even write to Valentine Knight to tell him you were going to have his child. Tony could have been a test-tube baby for all the rest of us knew of the man who sired him. It's a wonder you don't have a sign hung around the kid's neck saying "all my own work" and signed Karen Carne. Pride, that's your trouble—too much pride, and you're selfish into the bargain, not allowing a man to know or even acknowledge his own offspring.'

'I'm not selfish!' Karen flared, lifting her hair up from the back of her neck. Her hair felt heavy and her head was beginning to ache just like Mrs Craig's had been aching at the end of a long demanding day. Her lips twisted. Headache—the usual female complaint when the going got rough. 'It's been a hell of a day,' she continued, glaring at her sister. 'And I can do without you pointing out my shortcomings. We're doing a big promotion on that new woman writer and I've spent the day making sure everything is planned for next week. I'll be travelling with her right across the country next week. We fly out to Vancouver on Sunday, then work our way east as far as Halifax. Which reminds me, Mum, you'll look after Tony for me, won't you, please?'

'As usual,' sniped Iris. 'Supposing Mum said no for once, what would you do?'

'Ask you to look after him,' replied Karen, quick as a flash. 'And you know you'd agree to have him without hesitation.'

'Only because I love the kid and I'm sorry for him because he doesn't have a proper mother and father.'

'I am a proper mother!' the red-haired Karen flared up again.

'No, you aren't. Not to my way of thinking. And not to Mum's either. Aren't I right, Mum? Don't you think Karen should have got married when she knew she was going to have Tony and then settled down to stay at home and look after him?'

'Karen did what she thought she should do,' replied Pamela with cool impartiality.

'*Thought,* yes. But not what she *felt,*' said the sensitive yet easygoing Iris. 'Mind over matter, that's our Karen always, letting her head rule her heart.' She grinned at Karen, who frowned at her.

'I'll go and start getting the supper ready,' said Pamela, rising to her feet. 'Iris and Bill and the girls are staying to have the meal with us, Karen. Do you think I should plan on feeding Mr Knight too, when he comes back with Tony?'

'I don't know. You see, I . . . I'm not sure he'll be bringing Tony back,' faltered Karen.

'Of course he'll be bringing him back,' said

Pamela firmly. 'I expect he's taken him for a drive somewhere.'

'To McDonald's, is my bet,' said Iris with a laugh. 'Tony just loves to go to McDonald's. I guess because you never take him there, Karen. Just imagine, he'll come back full of hamburgers and Coke and will turn his nose up at Mum's lasagne.'

'Oh, shut up!' cried Karen, springing to her feet and snatching her jacket from the back of the chair. 'I'm going to bathe and change.' She followed her mother through the family room and into the kitchen. 'No supper for me, Mum,' she said. 'I've a date with Paul for dinner tonight.'

'And who will babysit the boy?' queried Pamela with silky sarcasm. 'I . . . or his father?'

'Now don't you start on me!' groaned Karen.

'Well, it would be nice, dear, if you could give me a little more notice when you want me to babysit. I could have had a dinner date myself this evening, couldn't I?'

'Yes, I suppose you could . . . and I wish you had.' Karen felt warm affection for her patient long-suffering mother flood through her and surprisingly gave in to it, putting an arm about Pamela's shoulders and hugging her. 'If you had a date I'd just have to phone around and find a baby-sitter, wouldn't I? Or stay at home with Tony and invite Paul to come here,' she said lightly. Then suddenly the anxiety she was feeling about Tony's disappearance broke through like a sharp jagged rock thrusting up through smooth waters. 'I wish I knew where Tony is,' she whispered. 'Oh, Mum, I wish I knew!'

'Now go and have your bath, dear,' said Pamela practically, although her brown eyes expressed sympathy. 'I'm sure they'll be back soon. As Iris says, they've probably gone for a drive. You know, Karen, it's only natural for a man to want to get to know his son; that is a man with anything about him, with any normal feelings—and Iris is right, you have been a little selfish over Tony. You haven't shared him with his father at all.'

'Because that was the way I thought Val wanted it to be,' Karen defended herself miserably. 'He said there were to be no strings in our relationship. We were both to feel free to change our minds about each other, to leave if we wanted to. That was why we didn't marry when we were living in London. He couldn't afford to be married, he said, and felt he wasn't able to take on the responsibilities marriage implies. And—well, I agreed. There was too much I wanted to do in life before being tied down in a serious relationship. But I've explained all this before. I explained to you when I told you I was pregnant and when we ran into Val three months ago in Maine. He and I are still free agents. . . .'

'No, you're not,' retorted Pamela, opening the oven and bending to peer in at the casserole she was cooking. 'Not any more. You have Tony to think of, and he needs a father as much as he needs a mother.'

'I know,' whispered Karen. 'And that's why I've decided to marry Paul.'

The oven door banged shut. Pamela swung

round to stare at her daughter with wide eyes.

'When?' she demanded.

'Soon. Maybe at Christmas. We haven't fixed a date.'

'But you've told Val?'

'Yes, I wrote to him three weeks ago telling him. He hasn't replied yet.'

'Until to-day,' said Pamela. 'His coming here to-day and picking up Tony from school is his reply, can't you see that? He wants his child.'

'Well, he isn't going to have him,' said Karen forcibly, and left the kitchen.

In the big double bedroom on the upper floor of the split level Karen tried to recapture her usual cool, sensible state of mind, to rule her heart with her head as Iris had accused her of doing. But it seemed her feelings and her imagination had got out of control.

Was it possible her mother was right, and was Val's sudden appearance in this suburb where he had never come before to pick up Tony from school his reaction to her letter informing him that she was going to marry Paul Dutton? She stared at the water as it swirled into the bathtub, wondering why she had written the letter in the first place. She was under no obligation to tell Val about anything that she wanted to do. No strings, that had been the basis of their friendship and their love for each other.

She turned off the bath taps, stirred the water with her hands to test the temperature and stepped into the bath. Lying down, she let the foam from the bubble liquid she had poured in cover her and resting her head in its waterproof shower bonnet against the back of the bath she closed her eyes and willed herself to relax.

When she had met Val for the first time both of them had been far away from their respective homes. They had both been living in London, England.

She had been sent to London by the publishing company she had been working for to spend a year in the editorial department of the company's British associate to learn the business of editing, and she had been there only a month when she had met Val in the editor's office, in the company's building on the South Bank of the Thames.

It had been a hot day in August and the windows of the third-storey office had been open, letting in the noise of traffic and the smell of exhaust fumes. James Lowry, the editorial consultant, who had been her boss at the time, had sent her to get coffee and she had been returning to the room carrying two mugs of milky liquid when she had first seen Val. Even now she could remember the heat, the noise, James Lowry's quiet English voice. . . .

The young man was tall. He stood before James Lowry's desk, his long jean-clad legs set wide apart, his arms folded across his chest, his dark longish hair sliding forward on to his forehead. Karen set a mug of coffee in front of James, who nodded but didn't stop talking, and went over to her own desk. Perching on the edge of it, she listened while she sipped her coffee.

The phone on James's desk rang. Still talking, he picked up the receiver, pressed a button and spoke into the mouthpiece. He listened for a few seconds, then said he'd be with someone in a minute and returned the receiver to its rest. He lunged to his feet.

'You'll have to excuse me,' he said, going round the desk and holding out his hand to the young man, who shook it. 'I hope you realise by now that I've nothing against the way you write. At the moment this company isn't considering going into that line of fiction, so I can do nothing for you except recommend that you try a publisher in your own country.' James turned to Karen, his broad homely face creasing into a smile. 'Karen, this is Valentine Knight. Remember that suspense thriller I gave you to read which you said set your hair on end? Well, meet the author of it.' James turned back to the young man. 'You and Karen have something in common as far as I'm concerned. You're both from the other side of the Atlantic. Find Mr Knight's typescript for him, will you, Karen, please? I have to go to a meeting.'

Coffee mug in hand, its contents spilling on the carpet, James lunged out of the room. Karen and Valentine Knight eyed each other warily. His eyes were a greenish grey, brilliant between thick black lashes, and it seemed to her that they sparkled like moss-covered stones seen under clear water. His lean face was pale and his hair was blue-black, thick and shiny, tumbling over his head in unruly waves.

'So you're from the other side of the ocean too,' he drawled, walking over to her and holding out a hand. 'Which part?'

'From Canada. My parents emigrated there from Britain when I was a baby. Actually I was born here in London. Where are you from?'

'From the States, but I've moved around a lot,' he replied casually. 'Are you going to find my manuscript for me?' he asked, obviously not in the least interested in the details of her background or in supplying information about his own.

'Yes, of course.' For some reason he disturbed her. Maybe it was the way his light eyes stared at her, seeming to look right through skin, bone and flesh; X-ray eyes zooming in on her mind. Slipping down from the desk, she went over to the filing cabinet where manuscripts which had been read but rejected were stored.

'Is your hair really that colour?' He spoke just behind her and she jumped, turning to look at him. He was very close and she could see a pulse leaping in the hollow of his throat. His blue denim shirt was open half way down his chest, not because he had left the buttons undone but because there were no buttons to fasten, and the opening revealed a mat of dark hair. His jaw was clean-angled, jutting forward determinedly, his nose straight and long and his brow, under the fronds of black hair, was broad and powerful, with two deep lines running straight across it. She guessed he was about twenty-eight or nine.

'Of course it is,' she retorted, turning back to the file and finding his manuscript. 'If I was going to dye my hair I certainly wouldn't dye it this colour.'

'But it's beautiful,' he murmured, and took hold

of one of the long ringlets which fell casually over
her shoulder. The hair coiled about his fingers like
a red snake. From looking at it he gave her an
underbrowed glance which made her nerves quiver
in a way that had never happened before, and she
drew her breath in sharply as if she had been
stabbed.

'Am I going to see you again?' he enquired softly,
and she found herself watching his lips. His thin,
hollow-cheeked face indicated a discipline and
asceticism that his lips belied. They had a generous
sensual curve to them.

'Do you want to see me again?' she whispered,
amazed that she of all people was involved in such
a passion-loaded, suggestive conversation.

'I do. When do you finish work to-day?' He took
the manuscript from her and tucked it under one
of his arms.

'Four-thirty.'

'I'll be waiting for you.'

He went from the room then, leaving her standing in a daze by the open filing cabinet. She spent
the rest of the day hazily, hardly aware of what she
was doing, thinking only of him, wondering
whether he had meant what he had said and looking forward, in spite of her innate caution, to four-
thirty. She did in fact skip out of the offices before
four-thirty, she was so eager to find out if he was
there, and he was, pacing up and down the busy
narrow sidewalk, as if he too were eager to see her
again. When he saw her he strode towards her, his
eyes lighting up, his hand reaching out to take hold
of her arms, and he kissed her full on the mouth,

careless of the raised eyebrows of surprised passersby. He kissed her as if they were lovers, and before too many days were over that was what they had become—lovers.

Karen opened her eyes, aware that the bath water was growing cool. Sitting up, she turned on the hot tap, then began to soap her skin. Falling in love the way she had fallen in love with Valentine Knight was something she had never expected to happen to herself. Since leaving school at the age of eighteen to go to work at the publishing company she had been friendly with several young men, but none of them had turned her on physically as her girl friends had assured her would happen if she ever fell in love.

Influenced by the contemporary trends in social behaviour, she had come to the conclusion that romance was non-existent, something that happened only in paperback novels. It was a snare and a delusion. She had also decided that marriage with all its attendant responsibilities of home-making and childbearing was not for her, at least not for a long time; not until she had made a career for herself and had achieved financial independence. She had made up her mind at twenty-two to stay single and free, doing what she liked when she liked. Never in her wildest dreams had she imagined she would fall in love as deeply as she had fallen in love with Val that year they had lived together in London.

She supposed that in a way it had been his attitude to love and marriage, so similar to her own, that had attracted her to him in the first place; that and the intense desire that had burned within him to succeed as a writer. Clever and ambitious, he had soon won her admiration and respect.

'I like you. I like you very much, and I'd like to live with you,' he had said to her on their third outing together. They had been sitting on the grass in Hyde Park which had been their favourite meeting place as it was for so many other loving couples. 'Would you be interested in living with me? The apartment I rent isn't very big, but there's room for two and it would be more fun to share it with someone like you. But I have to make it clear—there would be no strings.'

'No strings?' she had repeated in puzzlement.

'No tying of any knots to bind us to each other for ever. I can't afford to marry you. I'm a freelance writer trying to make the big time with a best-selling blockbuster of a suspense novel and apart from the money I earn from the occasional travel article or short stories I sell to magazines and a small legacy my mother left me when she died I have no steady income, so I can't afford to support a wife and children.'

He had turned to her, his hand reaching out to touch her throat within the curtain of her hair, his face coming nearer, his lips parting as they approached hers. 'What about you, Karen?' he had whispered. 'How do you feel about me, about us?'

'The same as you,' she had murmured shyly. 'I like you very much and I'd like to live with you, but I don't want any strings either. I don't want to marry yet. I'm too interested in making a career for myself. . . .'

He hadn't let her finish her sentence. Desire overwhelming him, he had claimed her lips in an erotic, sense-inflaming kiss which had told her much more than any words how he had felt about her, and later, from the park, they had walked through light-sprinkled dusky streets to his small two-roomed flat and it had begun that night, the passionate idyll that was to last almost a year.

Free love. Karen's lips twisted wryly as she stood up in the bath, water streaming from her white supple body, and reached for a towel. Oh, it had been truly free, she thought. Far away from her home, anonymous in the big, busy, most exciting metropolis in the world, she had felt free. The restraints imposed by family ties, by friends' criticisms, had fallen away from her. No one she knew in London had been in the least concerned that she and Val were living together.

Yes, they had been free, or had believed they had been. Free to love each other intensely and ecstatically. Yet they had been careful too, both of them taking precautions against the conception of a child until that last time when they had been together, when her emotions had been in a turmoil because she had had to fly back to Canada the next day, leaving Val for the first time since she had met him, and she had forgotten about everything except how much she had loved him and hadn't wanted to be parted from him.

Completely dry, Karen draped the thick bath-towel around her and went into the bedroom. Hearing the sound of a car turning into the drive-way, she went over to the window, standing to one side so that she couldn't be seen. Looking out, she felt disappointment stab through her. The car wasn't strange. It belonged to Bill Mather, Iris's husband—good, solid Bill to whom Iris had been married ten years; he always came home at the same time every night, a dependable and loving husband and father. Why had she ever thought him dull?

She turned to the wall-length closet where her clothes hung. She had so many clothes now it was often hard to decide what to wear. So different from that year in London when clothes had been the least of her and Val's concerns. Material possessions hadn't been important to either of them. Thoughts and feelings, and the sharing of them, had mattered most. Books, music, art came next. Oh, how they had talked and how they had shared ... everything, their innermost secrets, their dreams and their bodies.

Everyone at the publishing offices had been very kind to her the day she had received the news that her father had been seriously injured in a car crash and might die at any moment. James Lowey himself had made the reservation for her flight back to Toronto the next day and had sent her away at lunchtime to pack. Val hadn't been at the small apartment when she had arrived, but had come in later when she had been pushing the last of her belongings into her second case.

She had broken down while she had been telling him the news and he had taken her in his arms, pulling her down to sit on the bed with him, stroking her hair and not saying anything while she had sobbed. But slowly his caresses had grown more searching and titillating and their passion for each other had blazed up uncontrollably and more violently than ever before, consuming all caution, uniting them.

Yet next day they had been stiff with each other. Val had offered to go to Heathrow with her to see her off and she had refused, not wanting to say goodbye to him in that crowded place. Relief had been expressed clearly on his face and she could have cried out when she had seen it, guessing that he was glad she had refused.

'When will I see you again?' she had asked. The words *no strings* had been pounding through her mind.

'I don't know.' He had been standing with his back to her looking through the window, down at the street, watching for the taxi which she had ordered to come and take her to the nearest tube station. 'I had a letter from a New York publisher the other day. He's interested in publishing my novel and would like me to go and discuss it with him. I guess I'll fly over some time next week, as soon as I can sub-let this place.' He had paused and then had added tonelessly, 'The taxi is here. I'll carry the cases down for you.'

So in the end they had said goodbye on the pavement, kissing briefly before he had turned on his heel abruptly to walk back into the house and, numb with shock and misery, she had been driven away.

The sound of a car's engine idling before it was turned off sent Karen hurrying to the window again. Was it Val returning with Tony? She looked out and felt the cold prick of disappointment again. The car was parked in front of the next house and a woman was getting out of it.

Surely Val would bring Tony back soon? Her nerves twanging, Karen faced her reflection in the mirror. Her face was drawn into worry lines, making her look older than her twenty-nine years. What would Val think of her when they met? Although her figure was fuller than it had been seven years ago her face was thin. Gaunt, was Iris's unkind description of it. Gaunt, but interesting with hollows beneath the high cheekbones, dark shadows around the dark brown eyes. She was pale too, with being indoors too much. She had hoped to remedy that condition by going up to Paul's summer cottage this weekend. They planned to walk through the woods, to enjoy the brilliant fall colouring of the leaves, and to sit out on the sun-deck and sun themselves.

But if Val didn't bring Tony back she wouldn't be able to go.

She left the bedroom and went downstairs. Everyone was in the kitchen. Bill was mixing drinks. Iris was advising her two daughters on how to set the dining room table, while Pamela hovered over two pans simmering on top of the cooker.

'Hi, Karen. What will you have?' asked Bill. Fair and stockily built, he had blue eyes which crinkled at the corners when he smiled.

'Scotch on the rocks,' she said defiantly.

'Karen!' Pamela rebuked her quietly.

'Well, I need something to get me through the

next half hour while I wait for Val to bring Tony back,' Karen replied tautly. 'Where can they have gone? What does Val think he's doing?'

'Since none of us know him, none of us can guess,' said Iris jibingly. 'Perhaps Bill can enlighten us. After all, he's a man and a father. He might have some insight into the workings of the minds of his fellow men.'

'Mother knows Val. She's met him,' said Karen, taking a glass which clinked with ice from her brother-in-law. 'And she reads his books.'

'Don't you?' queried Bill.

'I . . . I read the first one,' she admitted coolly, looking down into the liquor in her glass.

'I've read them all,' continued Bill. 'That last one, *Brainchild*, was a real sizzler. I couldn't put it down, sat up all one night to finish it, didn't I, Iris?' He swallowed some of the liquor in his glass and then gave Karen a steady stare. 'If you really want my opinion, based on what I know of him through reading his books, I'd say he's taken Tony away with him.'

'But he has no right to take him anywhere!' Karen exclaimed. 'No right at all!'

'Only the right of being Tony's other parent,' Bill said quietly.

'But if he's taken Tony away with him without Karen's permission it amounts to kidnapping,' said Pamela. 'And although I didn't get to know him very well when Karen and I met him in June when we were in Maine, I don't think he would do anything criminal like that.'

'Desperate men often resort to desperate

actions,' murmured Bill musingly. 'Read *Brainchild* and find out. It's about a man trying to protect his daughter from a scientific organisation which is interested in using her psychic powers, and it shows how far a father is prepared to go when the child he loves is in danger.'

'But why should Val feel desperate?' demanded Karen.

'You should know,' drawled Bill, giving her a cold glance of open dislike that jolted her. 'You've denied him the chance to be a father to his own son.'

'Bill is right,' said Iris, appearing behind her husband's broad shoulder and placing an affectionate hand on it. 'You didn't even tell Val when you knew you were expecting Tony.'

'Why should I tell him? He was never interested in having a family. He made that quite clear from the beginning,' retorted Karen coolly.

'He wanted to marry you when you met him in Maine,' said Pamela, who was now serving up the meal. 'But you turned him down—I'll never understand why.'

'I refused because I guessed he only offered to marry me because he felt I expected it,' said Karen, slamming her empty glass down on the counter. 'And I wasn't going to be trapped into marriage to him just because I'd had his child.'

'There goes that pride again!' Iris sang tantalisingly. 'Come on, girls, help me carry the plates through to the dining room.'

Karen left the kitchen and went into the hall. It was nearly six o'clock. In an hour she was supposed to meet Paul in the city, but she couldn't possibly go until she knew where Tony was. She picked up the receiver of the telephone in the hall and dialled quickly. In a few seconds she was speaking to Paul.

'I can't meet you at seven,' she said, thankful he hadn't left his office. 'Something has happened and I'll have to wait here for a while to see if Tony comes home.'

'He's disappeared?' Paul sounded shocked.

'Yes.'

'Have you informed the police?'

'No, not yet. I ... I hope there won't be any need for that. Paul, do you think. . . .'

'I'll come there, as soon as I've finished some business, and you can tell me all about it then. See you about six-thirty to sevenish.'

'All right.'

She replaced the receiver and went back into the kitchen.

'Do you think there's enough left over for me?' she asked her mother. 'I'm not going out with Paul after all. He's coming here later.'

'Help yourself,' said Pamela, waving to the big casserole dish. 'And bring your own cutlery to the table.'

They had finished eating and Karen was helping Iris clear the table, carrying dirty plates back into the kitchen, when the phone rang. At once the hard fingers of fear clutched at her heart. Her glance went automatically to the clock on the wall. Twenty past six. The phone bell rang again. Neither Bill nor Pamela seemed disposed to answer it; Iris looked around from the sink where she was rinsing dishes ready for putting in the dishwasher. Karen walked over to the counter and put down the plates she was carrying. The phone rang again.

'Aren't you going to answer it?' said Iris.

Karen rubbed suddenly clammy palms against her hips and gazed appealingly at her sister.

'Please, Iris, you answer it.'

'Okay.'

The phone was ringing again when Iris picked up the kitchen wall receiver and said, 'Hallo.' She listened intently, frowning slightly, then looked across at Karen, holding the receiver against her chest so that whoever was on the other end of the line couldn't hear her.

'A man,' she whispered. 'He wants to speak to you.'

'Ask who he is,' muttered Karen.

Iris spoke into the mouthpiece, listened again, and then held it out to Karen.

'It's him,' she said. 'Here, take it.' She thrust the receiver at Karen, who took it in both hands, and went out of the room. For a few seconds Karen stared at the cream receiver, trying to compose herself. Then slowly she lifted it to her ear.

'Hallo, Karen Carne here,' she said.

'This is Val.' The tone of his voice was cool and noncommittal.

'Where are you?' she asked.

'In Bangor, Maine. We flew in from Montreal a few minutes ago.'

'Tony is with you?'

'He is. I picked him up from school at lunchtime.'

'You had no right to do that!' she exploded furiously. 'Bring him back at once. Bring him back home now!'

'No way,' he drawled. 'I'm taking him to my house to live with me there.'

'Where? Where are you going?' She was frantic now.

'To Seaton. I've bought a house near there, I'd like Tony to know about it and enjoy it.'

'Val, please listen to me. You've got to bring him back!'

'No. I only called you to let you know where he is and to tell you he's okay. Would you like to speak to him? He's right here beside me.'

'Yes. I would like to speak to him.'

There was a crackling sound, then Tony's voice, high-pitched and excited, shouted into her ear.

'Mummy, I'm with Val. He's taking me to his house by the sea.'

'You shouldn't have gone with him, Tony. He has no right to take you away from school.'

'But I wanted to go with him. Being with him is better than being in silly old school.'

'Tony, have you forgotten you and I promised Paul we'd go with him to his cottage tomorrow?' she persisted desperately, feeling for the first time since he had been born that she was totally out of touch with him. 'Don't you remember going there before and the good time you had with Paul, fishing on the lake?'

'I didn't have a good time with Paul. He shouted at me when I wouldn't do as he told me. Val says I can go fishing with him, and I like him better than Paul.'

'Tony, try to understand—that man who's taken you away isn't legally your father. . . .'

'He is, he is! I know he is—I look like him.' The boy's voice rose shrilly and there was another crackling sound as the receiver at the other end of the line changed hands.

'Val? Are you there?' Karen spoke sharply.

'Sure.'

'Why have you kidnapped him? He's my child. . . .'

'Mine, too,' he interrupted swiftly.

'But you don't have any legal authority over him.'

'I don't need it. My blood runs in his veins, and that's enough for me.'

'Oh, Val, please bring him back and we'll discuss the matter, make some arrangements for you to have access to him.'

'I don't want access to him. I want him to live with me all the time. I want to rear him, show him how to live.' He paused, then added coldly and clearly, 'If you want him back you'll come here and get him yourself.'

His receiver went down with a crash, and Karen was left listening to the dialling tone.

CHAPTER TWO

DAWN broke in the east, a pearling of the heavy clouds that shrouded the sky. Thick mist wreathed itself about the tops of the pine trees and hung in the branches of maples and birches. A few crimson and yellow leaves whirled slowly downwards to lie amongst the others already heaped beneath the trees. Some birds began to call to each other.

Karen opened her eyes and stared for a moment uncomprehendingly at the greyish-green gloom of the forest, wondering where she was and how she had got there. Her mouth felt dry and there seemed to be grit in her eyes. She rubbed her eyes with her knuckles and longed for a cup of good strong coffee.

Save for the cawing of crows it was quiet, the deep soft silence of the Maine woods. She glanced at her watch. Almost six o'clock. She had slept for nearly three hours, for it had been almost three when, after driving since eight o'clock the previous evening, she had pulled off the road into this logging road and had stretched out in the back seat of the car to sleep.

If she had planned this journey to Maine properly she would have made some coffee at home and brought it in a thermos flask to drink at this moment. But the journey hadn't been planned at all. At one point last evening, obeying some deep

34

inner urge, she had made up her mind that the only way to get Tony back was to do as Val had suggested to come and get him herself, and so she had walked out of the house, got into her car and had driven off.

Driving through the night across country along the highways and byways of northern New York State, Vermont and into Maine had certainly been preferable to staying at home to lie in sleepless torment in bed. The weather had been clear, the sky starlit, and for a short while there had been a moon shining down on the roofs of small towns, glinting on lakes and rivers, outlining trees and hills. Only as she had approached the coast had she run into swathes of fog drifting in from the sea along the river valleys.

She closed her eyes again, intending to sleep a little longer, until the day had begun properly and restaurants and gas stations in the next town would be open. Her mind wandered back to the previous evening when, shaking with a violence of disturbed emotions, she had hung up the phone in the kitchen and had gone through to the living room.

'What did he say? Is Tony with him?' Iris asked urgently.

'Yes, Tony is with him,' Karen replied, aware that Paul had arrived and was getting up from the armchair where he had been sitting.

'Where are they?' asked Pamela. 'Will they be coming back soon?'

'They're in Maine and they won't be coming back,' Karen replied dully.

'But he's all right? Tony is all right?' persisted Iris.

'He's all right. I spoke to him.'

'Karen, darling!' Paul was close to her and she lifted a cheek towards him for his kiss of greeting. 'You must be feeling sick with worry. Let me help. I can get on to the police right away and tell them Tony has been kidnapped. They'll contact the Maine police and they'll apprehend Knight. Do you know exactly where he's staying?'

'No. All I know is he's living near Seaton.'

Sleek and elegant in a beige pinstripe suit, his brown eyes gazing at her through the thick lenses of his glasses, Paul was supposed to be her friend in whom she could trust, yet for some reason she wished he hadn't come. She didn't want his help.

'What did you say the name of the place is?' asked Bill smoothly. He was taking a road map book from the book case.

'Seaton,' replied Karen.

'It's near Milworth,' said Pamela chattily. 'Karen and I stayed at an old inn near there nearly three months ago. That's where we met Valentine Knight. It was such a coincidence. The people who owned the hotel were putting on a luncheon for him. I spotted the poster as soon as we went into the hotel. It said "Come to lunch and meet Valentine Knight, the author of the best-selling spine-chiller *Dead of Night*"—that was his second book, you know? Of course I was delighted and wanted to go to the luncheon, but Karen wasn't at all keen, so she and Tony went off on their own somewhere. I know why now,' Pamela gave Karen a knowledgeable glance. 'She wanted to avoid seeing Valentine Knight. But he was still there when she came back and he recognised her. I think he recognised Tony was his son too. . . .'

'Mother, please!' Karen protested. 'Do we have to go over all that? Paul is hardly interested in what happened three months ago.'

'Kidnapping is a criminal offence,' said Paul in his precise lawyer's way. 'Knight could go to jail for taking Tony away from Karen without her permission.'

'But only if she presses charges, surely,' argued Bill in his calm solid way as he studied the map of Maine he had found, tracing the coastline with his forefinger. 'Is this the place, Karen?' he asked.

She sat down beside him on the chesterfield and looked at the blue and green map, at the criss-crossing of the red and yellow lines marking the roads. How far was it to Seaton from where she was? Near enough to a thousand miles, say eight hundred. If she set off now it would take her about eleven or twelve hours of continuous driving, all night and part of the morning. But she could do it. She had done it before, three months ago when her mother had wanted to go on holiday to Maine. And it would be better than lying awake sleepless in bed. It would be better than sending the police to look for Tony.

'Yes, that's the place,' she said in answer to Bill's question.

'It's so pretty there,' Pamela burbled. 'The inn where we stayed had been built in the early eighteenth century by a family who came from England to settle there, and the owner's wife was a relative of Valentine Knight's, I think. Karen, wasn't that young woman who did the cooking Mr Knight's cousin?'

'I believe she was,' Karen murmured, visualising Sue Allen. Was she still at the inn? she wondered. If she was she would probably know where Val was living.

'Karen, I think I should call the police,' said Paul, sitting down beside her. 'I know exactly who to contact to get things moving. Tony could be back here by tomorrow afternoon or Sunday at the latest if we put the police on Knight's tail.'

'No.' She turned to him urgently. 'I don't want the police in on this. Once we tell them there'll be publicity and I don't want Tony exposed to that sort of thing.'

'Then what are you going to do?' he exclaimed.

'Val said, on the phone, that if I want Tony back I have to go and get him myself,' she replied.

'But that's nothing short of blackmail!' Paul objected angrily. 'He'll be asking for a ransom next!'

'Blackmail or not, it's what I'm going to do. I'm going to get Tony myself. If I set off soon I'll be in Seaton early tomorrow and I can bring Tony back on Sunday.'

'By going yourself you'll be playing right into Knight's hands, can't you see that?' Paul was frowning at her. Suddenly he reached out and took both her hands in his. 'Darling, let me take care of this for you. I know the law. Knight has no rights over Tony, none at all.'

'Only the right of being the boy's father,' said Iris dryly.

'That would have to be proved,' Paul snapped at her.

'How?' countered Iris serenely, giving him look for look.

'Blood tests can be made.'

'Oh, his word isn't enough, then?' Iris raised her eyebrows.

'No, it isn't.'

'What about family resemblance?' queried Pamela. 'As soon as I saw Tony standing beside Valentine Knight I could see they were related. They have the same eyes.'

'And what about Karen's word?' said Bill. 'Surely that counts for something. She should know who sired her son. It isn't as if she's been the sort of woman who sleeps around with a lot of guys. . . .'

'Please, stop it!' Karen cried, springing to her feet. 'This . . . this whole affair has nothing to do with any of you! It's between me and Val, and I'm going now to drive to Maine to see him and talk it over, come to some arrangement like . . . like civilised people.'

'I'll come with you. I'll drive you,' said Paul, also rising to his feet. 'You can't drive all that way alone at night. You could have an accident miles away from anywhere. The car could break down when you're in the woods of Maine and you'd have to walk miles to get help. It's pretty wild and remote there. . . .'

'Look, I've been before,' said Karen tautly,

swinging round to face him. 'And I'm an adult woman and I've been looking after myself for a long time. I don't want anyone to come with me. I'm going alone and I won't have an accident and I won't break down. Is that clear?' Paul's face crumpled slightly and his eyes took on what she called secretly to herself their daffy expression. He looked hurt. She reached out a hand and placed it on his arm. 'I'm sorry, Paul, but this is something I have to do alone.' She smiled rather wryly. 'You could say it's my past catching up on me—a ghost which has to be laid, and only I can do the laying. Please try to understand.'

'But he might be violent, a little unstable. People who behave in this way, who kidnap children, often are,' he argued.

'That's a risk I'll have to take,' she said, turning to Bill. 'May I borrow your map book to take with me?'

'Sure,' said Bill, and for the first time in years he looked at her without hostility. 'I think you're doing the right thing, Karen,' he added, handing her the map book. 'And I wish you lots of luck.'

'Me, too,' said Iris ungrammatically, flinging her arms around Karen and hugging her. 'It's something you should have done long ago, only you were too damned proud and afraid to show your real feelings.'

'I'd willingly come with you, Karen,' said Pamela. 'But I know you want to see Valentine alone. You will drive carefully, won't you?'

Karen looked around at them, at her mother, her sister and her brother-in-law, her family, and felt that they were a hundred per cent on her side. At least she was doing something they approved of! Only Paul, the man she had promised to marry, had reservations. She glanced at him. He was still looking at her in that hurt way, as if she had suddenly developed into another person, one he didn't know or recognise.

'It will be all right,' she said to him, softly. 'I'll come back soon, with Tony.' She remembered suddenly the plans she had made to travel across the country during the next week. 'Oh, lord!' she groaned, hitting her forehead with the palm of her hand. 'Excuse me. I'll have to call Nita Rosen in the Public Relations Department and tell her I can't go with Margot Coventry to Vancouver on Sunday. Nita will have to take my place. . . .'

She had called Nita and after a certain amount of argument the woman had agreed to go on the publicity tour. Then she had packed a small overnight bag with a change of clothes and other necessities and had gone downstairs, ready to leave. Again Paul had offered to go with her, but she had been firm with him, assuring him that she would be safe and would return on Sunday with Tony. As she had backed out of the driveway he had followed her car and had had the last word, bending towards the open car window.

'Don't go, Karen, please. I have this gut feeling that you'll never come back. Or if you do that you won't be the same.'

She had given him a scathing glance and rolling up the window had driven forward and away down the avenue.

And now she was here, less than a hundred miles from her destination, short on sleep, feeling crumpled and gritty, but excited too. In another three hours, perhaps less, she would be in Seaton. She would go straight to the old inn overlooking the bay, hoping to find Sue Allen there, and she would ask Sue where Valentine Knight was living. She opened her eyes and looked out. Sunlight was shafting through the mist and the woods were aglow with its light. It was time to go. Opening the rear door of the car, she got out, stretched her arms above her head, took in deep breaths of the damp pine-scented air and then sliding behind the steering wheel she turned the key in the ignition.

Hills, covered with trees, the blue-green of majestic Weymouth pines, the scarlet of maple, the yellow of birch, flowed by as she drove along the winding grey road. Old farmhouses and barns, some painted white, some a silvery grey, appeared on clearings of land, tawny gold with the stubble left from hay-cutting or purple red with dying blueberry leaves. Wild asters and golden rod straggled beside fences and gates; chrysanthemums and late dahlias blazed in gardens. And beside each house were stacks of logs, already cut to size and split for use on the wood-stoves which warmed the old houses in the winter.

On the outskirts of Milworth in a shopping mall she breakfasted in a restaurant on blueberry muffins and coffee, then took another road, one which wound and twisted beneath tall drooping elms and beside a glinting blue river before lifting over rough barren land, a moonscape of huge granite boulders, glinting pink and grey in the sunshine. From that high place she could see the sea, misty blue, shimmering here and there with reflected sunlight, and scattered with small yellow and green islands. Then the road swooped downwards, past several elegant Colonial houses, all painted white and all with coloured shutters at their windows, some with brass eagles over the doors, and she was in Seaton, passing the general store, then the post office and the public library, and taking the road that forked left to follow the coast to the old inn.

The road ended in front of the long, low building of the inn, which was situated on a peninsula of land called Allan's Point. No other cars were parked before the hotel, nor were there any in front of the few holiday cabins which had been built in the field to the right of the house. As she approached the main door of the house Karen noticed the sign with the word CLOSED on it. Beneath the sign was another saying that the hotel would re-open the following May.

Going up to the nearest window, Karen shaded her eyes with her hand and peered in. The entrance hall looked just the same as it had when she had stayed at the hotel three months ago. There was the long refectory table, shining in the sunlight that slanted across it from a doorway opposite. There was a pottery bowl in the centre of the table with an arrangement of marigolds and dahlias in it. The flowers looked fresh, and that gave her hope. The hotel might be closed for the winter, but whoever owned it hadn't gone away yet.

From the back of the house came the sound of

hammering, so she walked round. Washing strung on a line fluttered in the sea-breeze. Against the house was a ladder, and at the top of it stood a man. He was replacing old shingles with new ones.

'Good morning,' Karen called up to him, and he stopped hammering to look down at her.

' 'Morning,' he drawled. Lean and long in faded workman's overalls, he slung his hammer into his belt to carry it and began to come down the ladder. When he was facing her she recognised him as the owner of the hotel, Titus Allan.

'You're Mr Allan?' she said, smiling at him.

'Sure am. What can I do for you?'

'I would really like to see your wife. Is she around?'

'Yeah.' He pointed to a screen door. 'Guess she's in the kitchen.'

Turning, he opened the screen door, then pushed the inner door open, put his head round and yelled.

'Sue, someone to see you!' He turned back to Karen, 'Go right in,' he said, standing back so she could step past him. 'She'll be with you in a minute.'

Karen thanked him and stepped into the big kitchen with its two big refrigerators, storage cupboards, double steel sink unit, central cooking range and festoons of copper, stainless steel and cast-iron pans. Footsteps sounded in the hallway and Sue Allan, small and neat, her brown hair arranged in a long braid, appeared in the doorway. She hadn't changed much since Karen had last seen her, and she stared at Karen with the pale Knight eyes, their clearness and coldness emphasised by the summer-ruddiness of her complexion.

'Hello,' Karen said. 'I don't suppose you remember me. My name is Carne—Karen Carne, and my mother and I and my little boy stayed here for a few days three months ago.'

Was it her imagination or did a shutter seem to come down at the back of those light eyes, and did Sue's pleasantly goodhumoured face stiffen a little?

'I hope you're not looking for accommodation,' said Sue in her quiet voice. 'We're closed. You'll probably get in at the motel outside the village. It's on the road to Milworth. . . .'

'No, I'm not looking for somewhere to stay,' Karen interrupted quickly. 'I'm looking for information. When we were here you put on a luncheon—it was a special occasion—so that people could come and meet Valentine Knight, the author. Do you remember?'

Sue's face didn't change expression. She continued to look at Karen with eyes that revealed nothing.

'Yes, I remember,' she said tonelessly. 'It was when we first opened and began serving lunches. We wanted to draw people's attention to the fact that there's an inn down here on the Point and that we do serve meals. Val . . . Mr Knight, that is . . . agreed to be present and to sign copies of his books. It was for publicity . . . for us and for him.'

'I realised that at the time, and it was a good idea,' said Karen. 'Somebody told me . . . that he's a relative of yours. Was that right?'

'He's my cousin and we grew up together, in the same town,' said Sue, still looking and sounding wooden.

'Then perhaps you could tell me where he's living now. I've heard that he's bought a house near here.'

Sue's glance wavered. It drifted over Karen's figure right down to her feet, then drifted slowly upwards again. Karen had the strangest feeling that she had just been assessed and found wanting.

'No, I'm afraid I couldn't tell you where he's living,' Sue said. 'He was here a few weeks ago, but I don't know where he is now. He moves around a lot.'

'But you know which house he has bought,' Karen persisted.

'I know, but I'm not going to tell you. He doesn't want everyone to know.'

'Oh, I see. But ... but ... it's very important that I know,' said Karen, realising suddenly that she was up against a blank wall. Sue Allan did not like her and would continue stubbornly to refuse to tell her which house Val had bought.

'Then go and ask someone else. I'm not betraying the whereabouts of Val's house to anyone. He asked me to keep quiet about it and so I am. Please excuse me now, I'm in the middle of painting one of the bedrooms and I'd like to get on with my work. Goodbye.'

Defeated, Karen left the kitchen and stepped out into the breezy sunshine. Titus Allan had disappeared, so she couldn't ask him. She had no alternative but to drive back to the village and ask there if anyone knew where Valentine Knight's house was.

The village general store had been remodelled on the lines of a supermarket with narrow lanes between walls of canned goods, packaged goods, jars of jelly, jam and relish, plastic-wrapped sliced loaves of bread. At a counter near the door an elderly woman was talking to the man who was behind the cash-register and nearby there was a revolving rack of paperback books. It didn't take Karen long to find the latest by Valentine Knight. Thick, with a cover designed in black and red on a white background, it had the number 1 in red on the top, indicating that it had been first on the best-sellers list.

She took the book over to the counter. The manager of the general store turned away from his gossiping customer towards her.

'I'd like to take this book, please,' said Karen, taking out her wallet. 'I've been told that Valentine Knight lives near Seaton. Have you ever met him?'

'Sure I have,' said the man. 'He comes in here all the time for his groceries.'

'Where does he live? I'd love to get his autograph,' said Karen gushily.

'He usually stays with his cousin, Sue Allan, down at the hotel on the Point,' said the gossipy customer. 'But he won't be there now.'

'But I'd heard he's bought a house near here,' said Karen, holding out her hand for her change. It seemed to her that the manager of the store had the same shuttered look she had seen on Sue Allan's face, meaning that he knew where Valentine lived but he wasn't going to tell anyone.

'Well, if he has, it's the first I've heard of it,' said the elderly woman customer. 'My son is the local town clerk and he knows immediately someone buys a house around here. Has to know who to send the bill to for the taxes, you know, and if Val Knight has bought a house in Seaton he'd tell me right off, so he would.'

Leaving the general store, Karen stood for a moment outside looking around wondering what to do next. After a while she decided to walk down to the fishermen's wharf. There was one boat in at the wharf and two men were unloading wooden crates. An older man was standing watching them. When he became aware of Karen he looked sideways at her and wished her good morning.

'Taking a late vacation?' he asked.

'You could say that,' she replied.

'Lovely weather for it.' His glance went to the book she was holding and pointed to it. 'He's just bought a house on one of the islands,' he said.

'Who has?'

'The author of that book. I saw him go out there last evening. Had a young boy with him.'

'How would he get there?' asked Karen. Excitement was racing through her again.

'Guess he has his own boat.' He came to stand beside her and looking out into the bay pointed to one of the islands. 'You see that island . . . the one with a humped back? That's the one. Big Spruce Island, it's called.'

'I'd love to go out to one of the islands,' said Karen. 'Are there any boat trips out there?'

'Not this time of the year. You're too late for that, but you could be asking Jerry over there if he'd take you for a ride. He'll do anything for a buck, will Jerry.' The old man laughed throatily, then raised his voice. 'Hey, Jerry—the lady here would like to go for a boat trip round the islands!'

One of the men, a bearded giant of a fisherman in a checked shirt and blue denim overalls, looked up, his eyes glinting in the shade of the visor of his cap.

'Cost you twenty bucks,' he said laconically, to Karen.

'How soon can we go?' she asked.

'Soon as you like,' he drawled.

'Good. I'll just go and lock my car.'

Fifteen minutes later, carrying her overnight bag over her shoulder, Karen stepped aboard the *Mary Lee*. The diesel engine started up with a roar, the ropes which tied the boat to the wharf were untied and thrown aboard and the forty-foot fishing boat sidled away from the wharf, turned and surged forward towards the distant islands.

'I really want to go to Big Spruce Island,' Karen shouted above the roar of the diesel engine to the bearded fisherman who stood casually turning the boat's wheel. 'I'd like to go ashore there.'

'You a friend of that writer guy?' queried Jerry, his small sharp blue eyes shrewd.

'Yes.'

'Okay, I'll take you to his dock. We'll be there in about fifteen minutes.'

Water rushed by, green and sparkling. Spray leapt up over the bow of the boat. The land, tawny brown and green, changed shape, and new headlands appeared. Then they were passed and the islands were coming closer, rising up out of the heaving shimmering sea, growing higher and wider, revealing details, rocky shores overgrown with seaweed, tiny yellow beaches, thick seemingly impenetrable woods of dark green spruce and twinkling silver birches.

Big Spruce was well named, because it was bigger than the other islands and was crowned with a forest of pointed, angular spruce trees. On the most westerly side there was a small bay protected by a reef of dark red rocks. The *Mary Lee* made straight for the reef and at the last minute slowed down and twisted sideways to slide through a narrow entrance into the bay.

'Here you are,' said Jerry as he took the boat close in to the wooden dock or jetty which jutted out from the shore. The boy who was helping leapt on to the dock and held the fishing boat casually by a rope.

'Thank you,' said Karen, and put a twenty-dollar note into Jerry's outstretched hand before she stepped over the wide bulwark of the boat on to the dock. The boy jumped back on board and just as Karen was going to ask Jerry to come back for her at about four o'clock in the afternoon the engine's throttle was opened and the fishing boat backed away. In a few seconds it was turning and surging towards the sea again. Water sucked and slapped at the pilings of the dock and the small open motorboat which was tied up danced on the wash created by the fishing boat.

Slowly Karen walked along the dock and along a well-beaten track that twisted through a jumble of yellowish grey rocks. Across a field overgrown with asters, golden rod and the remains of other wild flowers she walked towards an old fisherman's house which had clearly been renovated. Built in the simple maritime style, it had high gables at each end and was set at right angles to the bay and the prevailing winds. Its front was flat and had four windows in it, two upstairs and two down, on either side of a plain door which was closed. Karen, feeling again that unusual prickle of excitement dancing along her nerves, went up to the door and since there wasn't a door-knocker or a bell, rapped on the panels with her knuckles.

After knocking several times without obtaining an answer she gave up and stepped through the overgrown grass and dying golden rod to the nearest window to look through it. She looked into a room which was furnished with an antique dining set, a long table with Windsor-backed chairs placed around it. In one corner of the room was a spinning wheel. Old china glinted on a dresser with an open hatch.

Leaving that window, Karen went over to the one on the other side of the door and peered through it, and was immediately satisfied that she had come to the right house. Furnished as a sitting room, it was being used as a study and on a big desk placed against a blank wall was a typewriter. Books, piles of them, were scattered across the floor and there were sheaves of paper lying on the desk. The chair at the desk was pushed back just as if someone had left it.

She stepped away from the window and felt the hairs on her neck prickle warningly. She swung round quickly, her glance darting about, convinced that someone was watching her. But there was no one walking up the path from the shore and no one standing on the edge of the cliffs in front of the house and no one, as far as she could see, among the dark trees to the left.

The grass rustled in the light breeze. Down on the shore waves whispered against the shingle and amongst the rocks. In the distance the *Mary Lee*'s engine droned as the fishing boat made its way back to Seaton Harbour. Otherwise there was silence.

Turning again to to the door, Karen pounded on it and this time when no one answered it she turned the knob and pushed. The door opened easily and she stepped cautiously into the small square entrance hall from which the stairs rose straight up in front of her to the second floor. She closed the door and went into the room where the desk and typewriter were and from there through another doorway into the kitchen at the back. It had been fitted out with all modern equipment and on the counter beside the sink dishes, which had been rinsed, were stacked in a drainer. Karen stood for a moment looking around for signs that Tony had been there, but found none.

She left the kitchen, going through to the dining room and out again into the small hallway. Up the stairs she climbed to the upper storey. Once she guessed it had been two big areas divided by the stairwell. Now it was divided into three rooms, two bedrooms and a bathroom. In the biggest room at the front there was a double bed, unmade, across which were thrown a man's pyjamas. In one of the smaller bedrooms a pair of Tony's socks, the ones he had worn the previous day, lay on the mat beside the bed.

Karen picked up the socks and sat down on the edge of the single bed. Where was Tony? He had been here, had presumably slept in this bed, but he wasn't here now, nor was Val. Yet they must still be on the island; if they had left it the motorboat would not have been tied up at the dock.

A wave of weariness washed over her suddenly and she gave in to it, keeling over on her side, laying her head on the pillow where Tony's head had rested, lifting her legs and curling them up. She would rest while she waited for them to come back to the house. They would come back for lunch, surely. She yawned as she glanced at her watch. It was almost noon. In a few minutes they would return and she would see Val again. How would he look? How would he behave when he saw her again? Her eyelids drifted down over her eyes and she imagined she was at the inn, three months ago, returning with Tony, stepping into the entrance hall of the hotel. . . .

Seeing the tall man with the black hair talking to her mother, Karen pulled up short and would have retreated through the front door of the hotel again, taking Tony with her. But the boy made any retreat impossible. Noticing his grandmother, he wrenched his little hand from Karen's and scampered across the polished wooden floor.

'Gran, Gran, look what I've brought for you!' He held up the bunch of wild flowers he and Karen had picked and tugged at Pamela's skirt.

'How nice, dear.' Pamela smiled down at him, ruffled his black hair and took the flowers from him. 'Thank you.' She looked up at Valentine Knight, who was staring down at Tony. 'This is my grandson Tony, Mr Knight.'

'He's staying here, alone with you?' Valentine's voice was hoarse and he looked directly at Pamela, whose brown eyes blinked bemusedly before their glance slid down to Tony, then up again to the man's face.

'No. My daughter Karen is here too. She's over there, by the door.'

As Valentine turned quickly Karen wrenched open the door behind her and stepped outside. Her heart was racing madly, filling her ears with its noise. Walking quickly, she went round the corner of the house and across the field at the back, which sloped down to the shore of the bay, not stopping until she reached the beach of shingle which curved round to a rocky headland, and even there she didn't stop but kept on, climbing over the rocks.

'Karen, wait!' Valentine's voice was breathless behind her. Surprised, she half turned, her right ankle gave way and with a little yelp of pain she lost her balance and fell down. On her bare arms his hands were warm, lifting her to her feet.

'What happened?' he asked.

'My ankle twisted,' she whispered. She put her right foot down slowly. Pain needled upwards from her ankle, then faded. 'It's all right now. You can let go of me. I can stand unsupported.'

'You're sure?'

'Yes.' She raised her eyes to his face. More in control of herself, she was able to look at him steadily and coldly. Slowly his hands slid from her arms. Still staring at her, he folded his arms across his chest and his mouth curved into a slight, smile.

'It's been a long time,' he drawled. 'All of seven years, I think. How are you, Karen?'

'Well, thank you. And you?'

'Pretty good. Quite a coincidence meeting your mother at the lunch today.' He paused, then added softly, 'Then meeting her grandson, Tony.' The pale eyes became sharp, seemed to bore right into hers. 'He's my son as well as yours, isn't he?'

'How did you guess?' she retorted flippantly, beginning to walk away from him, back across the rocks towards the beach.

'Why didn't you tell me you were pregnant?' he demanded harshly as he followed her.

'Because I didn't know until three months after I'd left London. Anyway, you'd said you didn't want any strings, and since you didn't write to me and I had no idea where you were or how to get in touch with you, I assumed you wouldn't be interested.'

Fingers bit into her arm, bruising the soft flesh above the elbow, and she was swung round to face him. His eyes glittered with livid light.

'You dared to assume that I wouldn't be interested in the birth of my own child, in my own flesh and blood?' he said through thinned lips. 'My

God, I would never have believed you could be so arrogant! You should have let me know.'

'How? Tell me that?' she retorted 'What was I supposed to write on the envelope—Valentine Knight, care of New York, U.S.A.?'

He flinched as if she had hit him and his hand dropped to his side.

'Okay, I guess I was in the wrong and I should have written to you, let you know where I was,' he said bitterly. 'The truth is I didn't write because. . . .' He broke off, his face stiffening with pride, and gave her an underbrowed searching glance. 'It must have happened that last night we were together,' he said quietly, 'when you were so upset about your father.'

Karen didn't reply but started to walk on again, jumping down from the rocks to the shingle beach. The tide was coming in, the water rushing in little waves that tumbled on to the shore then spread outwards, only to slide back again.

'Did you ever receive the copy of my first novel that I sent to you?' Val asked, catching up with her, his long legs clothed in straight-cut trousers of navy blue twill striding beside hers.

'Yes, I did.'

'Then you could have written me care of the publisher. You could have let me know that Tony had been born.' Again his voice grated harshly, and she stopped walking to turn to him, her back to the moving sunlit sea.

'Supposing I had told you, what would you have done?' she challenged.

'I'd have come to you,' he replied, facing her, his

hands on his lean hips. For the lunch he had dressed neatly and conventionally in a blue and white checked shirt and a grey tweed jacket. His hair, although still thick and longish, was not as long as it had been when she had known him in London, and the shorter cut made him look older, less Bohemian and casual, more responsible. But then he was older—thirty-five to her twenty-nine. 'I'd have asked you to marry me,' he added, bending towards her so he could look directly into her eyes, his own alight with little green flames.

She stepped back, afraid of that look, afraid of the way her pulses leapt in response to it, and turning on her heel she strode onwards, shingle crunching under the soles of her sandals and sliding over the sides of them to scrape and irritate her bare feet.

'Karen, for God's sake, why didn't you let me know?' he demanded harshly, catching up with her again.

'I didn't need you,' she lied breathlessly. 'I was quite capable of having a baby, of looking after and rearing a child by myself. Other women have done it in the past and in the present, very successfully, and I decided I could too. I didn't need a husband or a partner.'

'But I had a right to know,' he insisted.

'No, you didn't. We didn't have any rights over each other,' she retorted, still hurrying on.

'So this meeting here today really is a concidence. You didn't know I would be here in Seaton.'

'I didn't know until Mother saw the advertisement for the lunch.'

'Sue asked me to come to help her launch her new lunch programme and put the inn on the map,' he explained. 'It was the least I could do for her and Titus.'

'You've become a celebrity,' she mocked gently. 'With your most recent book at the top of the best-sellers list for six weeks, you're the local boy who's made good, and Sue must be pleased with the numbers of people you attracted to the inn today. I was hoping you'd have gone by the time Tony and I came back and that you wouldn't see him.'

'And then I'd have never known I have a son, I suppose,' he said bitterly. 'My God, how you must hate me!'

'No, I don't—truly I don't,' she hastened to assure him, turning to him, her hands going out appealingly. He caught them in his and turned them over, examining the fingers.

'You aren't married,' he said, noting her ringless fingers.

'No. Are you?'

His eyes steady on hers, he drew her slowly towards him.

'No.' He shook his head. 'Karen, we could marry now, to give the boy a stable home background.'

'No, no!' She pulled her hands free of his grasp. 'I don't want to marry for that reason,' she cried, backing away from him. 'I don't want to marry you. Goodbye, Val. We're leaving in the morning, so I won't see you again.'

She began to hurry towards the hotel. Again he caught hold of her arm and swung her round to face him, jerking her against him. His arms went around her, his hand forced her chin up and his mouth closed over hers.

The pressure of his lips was a deliberate provocation, a reminder of the sensual pleasures they had enjoyed together once, and for a moment, unexpectedly, her senses swam giddily her lips opened to the probing of his and her breasts tautened beneath her sweater. Then her reason spoke coldly and clearly to her, warning that he was using his knowledge of her response to his lovemaking in the past to persuade her to give in to him and agree to marry him. Using all her strength, she pulled her lips from his and pushed him away.

'Tony has a stable home background,' she said coldly. 'He doesn't need you, nor do I. Goodbye.'

She turned away again and walked up to the hotel. Val didn't follow her and she didn't see him again. The next morning she and Pamela and Tony set off early to begin their journey back home. They had driven almost a hundred miles before Pamela referred to Valentine Knight. Then she said quite abruptly,

'Why didn't you ever tell us that Valentine Knight is Tony's father?'

Karen's foot faltered on the accelerator. The car slowed down, wandered about the road a little as she gave her mother a surprised sidelong glance.

'How do you know he is?' she exclaimed.

'Before you came back to the hotel yesterday he told me he'd known a young woman from Canada called Carne when he lived in London a few years back. He wondered if she could be some relative of mine. He said her first name was Karen. I kept him talking until I was sure you would be back so that I could see how he reacted when he saw Tony and how you would react when you saw him.'

'Mother! I didn't think you could be so cold-blooded and calculating,' Karen chided mockingly.

'Oh, I can do anything when I feel that the happiness of a member of my family is at stake,' retorted Pamela.

'And who's unhappy?' queried Karen lightly, keeping her glance fixed ahead on the road which dipped up and down as it crossed the vast expanse of Maine countryside rolling away into the distance, a mass of green trees broken here and there by a flash of blue water where there was a lake.

'You are, for one. You have been for years. That's why you drive yourself at work so much; why you're always dashing off to meetings, staying late at the office. You can't bear to be still or alone. You can't live with yourself.'

'That isn't true!' protested Karen hotly. 'I work hard because I like my job. I like it more than anything else in the world.'

'More than Tony?' said Pamela dryly.

Again the car wandered about the road a little as Karen glanced at her mother uneasily.

'I have to work to support him,' she argued, 'but that doesn't mean I don't love him and want the best for him.'

'Then why haven't you let him have a father?' asked Pamela in her deceptively placid way. 'Why have you never given Valentine Knight a chance to be his father?'

'Because Val always said he didn't want to be tied down. He said marriage would come between him and his ambition to be a writer. I didn't tell him Tony was born because I didn't want him to feel I expected him to marry me. And I still don't want him to feel that way. He's free to live the way he wants and I'm free to live the way I want.'

'Love is never free,' remarked Pamela with the comfortable wisdom of the middle-aged woman who has loved and been loved in return, has been happily married and has had children and reared them. 'Someone always has to pay in the long run. You're making Tony pay for the free love you enjoyed with Valentine Knight by not letting him grow up with his father.'

'Oh, I didn't expect you to understand, 'Karen burst out miserably. 'Let's talk about something else, please.'

But the meeting with Val had disturbed her, and she had been even more disturbed when she had received letters from him during the next few weeks, reiterating his proposal of marriage and hinting that he would be coming to see her and Tony soon. She hadn't replied to the letters. Only after she had agreed to marry Paul had she written, and as a result of that letter she was here, lying on the bed where Tony had slept the previous night and waiting for him and Val to return.

She yawned again. The silence of the house and the warmth of the room were relaxing. The sleepless hours of the night caught up on her and she sank into a deep dreamless slumber.

CHAPTER THREE

'HEY, look who's sleeping in my bed, Val!' The boy's treble voice squeaked with surprise. 'How did you get here, Mummy?'

Karen opened her eyes and blinked bemusedly at Tony, who was standing beside the bed staring at her, his grey eyes wide with amazement. He reached out a hand and touched her face with grubby sticky fingers as if to make sure she was real, then leaned forward and gave her a sloppy kiss on the mouth. She smiled at him.

'Hi, darling,' she said.

'What are you doing in my bed?' he asked.

'I've been resting. I've come to take you back home with me.'

The expression on his face changed from puzzlement to wariness. He stepped back quickly from the bed, his dark eyebrows slanting in a fierce frown.

'No, no, I don't want to go back home with you. I want to stay here,' he said excitedly. 'Val says I can stay here. He say I can live with him all the time. He says you can stay too, Mummy.'

Rejection of any suggestion of hers by her child was new to Karen. Usually Tony was only too glad to go anywhere with her, possibly because he saw so little of her. His attachment to her was something she valued highly and she had assumed he would be ready to return home with her when he saw her.

Supporting herself on one arm, she pushed her sleep-tangled hair back from her face. Val had come into the room and was leaning against the door jamb. His black hair was windblown, tumbling in shiny waves over his head, and his long-jawed face was tanned to the colour of golden teak so that his greenish-grey eyes looked pale in contrast. Both hands thrust into the pockets of the navy blue denim trousers he was wearing, he looked at her with interest, his glance wandering from her face over her body to her long, nylon-sheathed legs. Her skirt had ridden above her knees while she had slept and a good part of her thighs were on show, softly rounded, their white skin shining seductively through the fine beige mesh. Suddenly selfconscious under his probing stare, she twitched the skirt down and swinging her legs over the edge of the bed sat up straight.

'It's good to see you, Karen,' he said, his voice lilting in the lazy drawl which had always fascinated her. 'How did you get here?'

'I drove down last night and arrived in Seaton about ten this morning. A fisherman called Jerry brought me out to the island.' She glanced at her watch and saw with dismay that it was nearly four o'clock. She had slept more than three hours. 'Oh, it's time we went back!' she gasped.

'We?' queried Val, raising his eyebrows.

'Tony and I,' she replied crisply. 'That's why I've come, to take him back home with me. You said that if I wanted him back I was to come and get him myself, so I've come. You can't keep him here on this island. He has to go to school on Monday.'

'But I don't want to go back,' complained Tony. 'I'm not going back. I want to stay with Val.' He scowled at her again. 'You can't make me go back, Mummy.'

Over Tony's head of tousled black hair Karen looked at Val, her glance fiercely accusing. He looked back at her with a glint of humour in his eyes as his mouth curved into a mocking grin.

'How are you going to get back to Seaton?' he asked smoothly. 'Is Jerry coming for you?'

Her glance wavered away from his and she bit her lip in annoyance with herself for not having asked Jerry to come back to the island for her.

'No, he isn't,' she muttered.

'So how are you and Tony going to get back to Seaton?' Val persisted.

'Don't you have a boat?' she asked, looking up at him.

'I do, but I'm damned if I'm going to take you and Tony over to the mainland today.'

'But you must,' she insisted, rising to her feet. 'Tony, where's your jacket?'

'I dunno. I forget,' said the boy surlily, his lower lip pushing out stubbornly as he glared at her from under lowering eyebrows. 'And I'm not going with you. I'm staying here with Val. You can't make me go with you. You can't, you can't!' His voice rose to a shout and whirling round he rushed out of the room.

'Tony, come back here!' Karen snapped, and

lunged towards the doorway to follow him, only to find herself in collision with Val's lean hard body as he stepped in front of her. 'Oh, get out of my way!' she stormed at him, and beat at him with her fists as he took hold of her arms to steady her. 'Stand aside and let me go!'

'Not until I know what you intend to do to Tony if you catch him,' he retorted.

'Oh!' she gasped, pulling free of his grasp and stamping a foot on the floor in frustration as she heard Tony's footsteps thumping down the stairs. She glared at Val accusingly again. 'See what you've done by bringing him here with you?' she raged. 'You've confused him and he doesn't know how to behave any more. I suppose you've told him that you believe that living here on an island with you, free from rules and regulations, is a much better way to learn than going to school is.'

'No, I haven't told him that ... yet.' His mouth curled in sardonic appreciation of her indirect reference to the views he had held about compulsory education seven years ago when he had lived in London. 'But I could and I will if you persist in saying you're going to take him away with you.' He leaned against the door-jamb again, tipping his head back and studying her from beneath drooping eyelids. 'You haven't guessed yet why I went to his school and brought him away with me, have you?' he challenged.

'You've done it to to torment me,' she replied.

'Not to torment,' he drawled, shaking his head, 'but to get your attention. It was the only way I could think of to get you to meet me. I guessed that in spite of appearances to the contrary the maternal instinct in you is as strong as the paternal instinct is in me and that you would soon come flying after your duckling to make sure he's safe and not being led astray by the wicked ideas of the man who's his father.' The greenish-grey eyes glinted with mockery again as he leaned towards her. 'And I guessed right, didn't I? You came, you're here, and you're going to stay for a while, my love.'

'Don't call me that,' she muttered between set teeth. 'I'm not *your* love.'

'I'll be the judge of that,' he retorted, pushing away from the jamb and stepping towards her. 'I'll decide for myself which woman qualifies for the position of being *my* love.' He stood over her and suddenly the old familiar sensual magic weaved itself about her, ensnaring her. Her legs lost the will to move, her breath caught in her throat and a slight sweat broke out on her skin as the heat of physical desire pulsed through her unexpectedly. She couldn't find the power to step away from him or even around him. He raised a hand and touched her hair at her temple lightly.

'It's still a beautiful colour, hasn't faded at all,' he murmured, reminding her deliberately of the excitement and enchantment of their first meeting. His dark lashes flicked up and he looked into her eyes, his own warming with a smile. 'You've worn well over the years, sweetheart,' he continued softly, and she felt her knees shake. 'There aren't too many lines on your face and its seems to me that your figure is fuller, more curvaceous, than it used to be, improved by childbearing. I'm glad my trick to get you to come here worked and that you've come.'

'I'm not staying,' she said, making her voice cold and flat, trying not to show how much he was disturbing her. She pulled her hair free of his fingers and tucked the strand behind her ear.

'Of course you are going to stay,' he replied. 'It's very comfortable here, quiet and peaceful too. I've stocked up on food and there's enough gasoline to keep the generator going for electricity, enough wood split to keep the stove going. We're completely self-sufficient here, like all the other islanders.'

'Oh. Then there are other people living on this island?' she said quickly and hopefully.

'Sure, there are, most of them fishermen although there are a few artists too. We'll have a few days here together, the three of us, getting to know each other so that we can come to some arrangement for living together on a more permanent basis.'

'I'm not going to marry you, if that's what you mean by arrangement,' she replied tautly. 'I'm going to marry Paul Dutton at Christmas.'

'Not if I can prevent it,' Val retorted, his eyes losing their warmth and glittering with a frosty light. 'I'm not having my son brought up by a stranger.'

'Paul isn't a stranger to Tony,' she argued. 'You are the stranger. Tony has known Paul longer than he's known you.'

'And doesn't like him,' he said dryly.

'That isn't true! You're making that up. How can you possibly know how Tony feels about Paul?'

'I know because he told me on the way here. He told me that you're going to marry a man he doesn't like. He told me he doesn't want Paul to be his stepfather.'

'Tony would never think of saying that by himself. You must have put the idea into his head,' she accused.

'You have a very high opinion of my abilities to influence a strong-willed six-year-old boy,' he drawled.

'I know how clever you are with words and how persuasive you can be. I know you were able to convince him that it was all right for him to leave school with you and come here. I know you were able to persuade a hard-headed man like Mr Mackindall, the principal of the school, to let Tony go with you,' she retorted shakily, knowing that Tony had always behaved badly in Paul's presence and possibly did dislike him.

'If you persist in marrying Paul you'll lose Tony, you know,' Val said calmly and reasonably. 'And don't ask me how *I* know. He's my flesh and blood and he'll behave as I did when my mother married a man I didn't like. He'll clear out and run away from you, and now that he knows about me he'll come to me.'

'Did you go to your father when you ran away from your mother?' she asked curiously. She hadn't known until now anything about his family background, because he had never talked about family when she had lived with him in London and she had always had the impression that he was a loner, completely without close friends or relatives.

'I couldn't because he was dead,' he replied tersely.

'Then what did you do?'

'I went to my father's brother's home in Portland. You've met my cousin Sue Allan. I lived with her family until I was able to make it on my own.'

'Didn't you ever go to see your mother again?'

'Not while she was married to that man,' he replied curtly. 'Not until after she found out what he was like and left him.'

'Tony would never be like that,' Karen whispered. 'He could never be so cruel . . . to me.' Her head went back and she glared at him defiantly. 'But if he does run away and comes to you I'll sue you for something, kidnapping or something. Paul's a lawyer and he'll advise me.'

'And if you do that I'll smirch your reputation so much in court that no judge will consider you suitable to be a mother,' he threatened silkily, stepping close to her again. 'Think of that, Karen. Think of how clever I am with words and my powers of persuasion. Think of what I could tell a court about you and me, in London; about how we lived and loved together, how circumstances separated us and how you neglected to tell me you were expecting my child; how you've denied me the right to be a father to my own son.'

'You wouldn't!' she protested in a whisper, staring at him in horror.

'Of course I would. I'll do anything to get the custody of Tony if you insist on marrying another man while I'm alive.'

The ring of sincerity in his voice, the intense expression in his light eyes which seemed to blaze with pale greenish fire, caused her to back down temporarily from the position she had taken. Pushing her hands into the slit pockets of her suit skirt, she studied Val from under her lashes.

Physically he had changed slightly too. He wasn't as thin as he had been seven years ago and the aura of self-confidence which she had sensed about him the last time they had met had increased. It was true the lines across his high forehead and about his wide mobile mouth had deepened and that there were some threads of silver in the black hair which was swept back from his temples, but otherwise he had worn well over the years too, and he was still as sexually attractive to her as he had ever been.

'You seem to have changed your views on life since we lived in London,' she taunted lightly. 'Remember you believed in free love, in no strings and no responsibilities?'

'I remember. I've never forgotten, but I was beginning to think you had. I remember that you held the same views I did and that was why you were willing to live with me. Neither of us wanted commitment then. Neither of us wanted responsibilies and we had no intention of bringing a child into the world.' His face hardened and his eyes narrowed. 'Sure, I've changed my views. You see, I found out that there's no such thing as free

love after a...
pay for loving...
think you have...

'Yes, I have. ...
him up on my ...
'That's the price I've ...

'What mistake?' He...

'The mistake I made...
when you asked me to li...
remembering as if it had...
before the pain she had fel... ...her
leave him so easily. Turning ...ked up
her suit jacket from the chair w... ...had laid it
before she had lain down on the ... . She put it on
and turned round to face him again. 'You have no
legal right to take custody of Tony,' she said. 'He
doesn't even bear your last name.'

'Only because you refused to let me have that
right,' he replied coolly. 'But you can give me that
right very easily. You can marry me, Karen. I've
asked you several times during the past months.
You can marry me, as you would have married me
if I'd been able to ask you nearly seven years ago,
if you'd let me know you were expecting my
child.'

'No, I can't,' she muttered. 'I can't marry you.'

'Why not?' he demanded.

'Because . . . oh, because I've promised to marry
Paul, that's why, and I . . . I . . . well, I don't break
promises.'

'Are you in love with him?'

'I. . . .' Her glance wavered away from the sharp-
ness of his gaze. 'I don't know,' she replied.

...you promised to marry
...arshly.
...asons which you would never
...because I'm tired of being on my own;
...Tony needs a father; because Paul is in
...with me,' she replied rather wildly as she
looked round and found her overnight bag and
slung it over one shoulder. She walked towards the
doorway. When she was level with him she stopped
and looked up at him again. His face had gone
pale under the tan and his lips were gripped tightly
together as if he were holding back some abrasive
wounding remark. 'I'm not staying a few days here
with you. I'm going back to Seaton,' she said
firmly. 'And since you won't take me I'll go and
ask one of the island fishermen to give me a lift in
his boat.'

'Then you'll go without Tony,' he said coldly,
and went through the doorway ahead of her.

'But you can't keep him here. You can't!' she
argued, and broke off, realising she was shouting
after him in much the same way as Tony had
shouted at her before he had rushed from the room.
Her lips tightening, she left the bedroom and
marched along the landing and down the stairs.
Val had gone. He wasn't in the hallway, nor was
he in the study, but there was someone in the kitchen, because she could hear movements. She
walked across the study to the doorway and looked
into the kitchen, fully expecting to see Val with
Tony. Instead she saw a tall well-built young
woman of about twenty-two or three who was
standing at one of the counters rolling pastry

dough and humming along to the Country and Western music which was coming over a small transistor radio.

'Excuse me,' Karen said loudly as she advanced into the kitchen. 'Have you seen Mr Knight?'

The young woman whirled round so that her straight silky blonde hair that hung almost to her waist flirted out. Rolling pin in one hand, she stared at Karen with wide blue eyes, her full-lipped mouth hanging slightly open in surprise.

'I'm sorry,' Karen forced herself to smile, 'I didn't mean to scare you.'

'I didn't know there was anyone else in the house,' replied the young woman, putting down the rolling pin and picking up a cloth to wipe flour off her hands. 'Have you just come? Were you knocking at the front door? I didn't hear you.' A smile curved her lips, showing that she had big white teeth, and she reached out a hand to turn down the volume of the radio. 'I guess no one could hear anything through that racket,' she said dryly.

'No, I haven't just come. I came a few hours ago,' replied Karen. 'I've just been talking to Mr Knight and. . . .'

'He went out.' The young woman half-turned her head to look out of the window behind her. Her profile, broad brow, turned-up nose and rounded chin, was clearly etched against the light. 'I don't see him now. He asked me if I knew where Tony had gone. I told him the boy had gone out, so he said he'd go and look for him.' She looked back at Karen. 'Tony is his son, you know, and has come to live here.'

'I know,' said Karen tartly. 'I'm Tony's mother, Karen Carne. Who are you?'

Curiously and objectively she watched shock go through the young woman in reaction to her announcement that she was Tony's mother. The round blue eyes widened even further and the smooth suntanned cheeks went pale, then flushed bright red.

'I'm Laurie—Laurie Arnold. I've been keeping house for Val all summer and I came over here after lunch in my father's pick-up truck.' She paused, gave Karen a swift assessing look, then added in a rush, 'I didn't know Val had a wife.'

'He doesn't. He and I aren't married,' said Karen smoothly.

'Oh, I see.' Laurie's face slackened with relief. 'You and he are divorced?'

'No. We've never been married.' She might as well tell the truth, thought Karen, so that there wouldn't be any misunderstandings, and she watched the red tide of embarrassment wash over Laurie's face again. 'Do you live on the island all the time, Laurie?' she asked pleasantly in an attempt to help the young woman over the uncomfortable moment.

'My folks do. My father is a fisherman and my mother keeps the general store in the village at Green Cove—that's on the other side of the island where it's more sheltered,' replied Laurie, relaxing again. 'But I've lived mostly on the mainland since I started going to school. I came back to the island this summer when I graduated from the State university and Val asked me if I'd like to work for him for a while. I haven't been able to find a permanent job yet, so I stayed on here this month.' She grinned rather selfconsciously. 'I'd like to be a writer too and I'm hoping to pick up some tips from Val. He and I hit it off together really well.' She gave Karen a sly sidelong glance. 'Are you going to stay here long?' she asked.

Meaning; *I hope you're not going to stay here long so that I can have Val to myself again*, thought Karen wryly.

'No, I'm not staying,' she replied. 'As soon as I can find someone to take me back to Seaton I'm leaving and taking Tony with me.'

'Is Val going to take you to Seaton in his boat in this weather?' exclaimed Laurie, glancing out of the window again. 'He's crazy if he does. That little scallop shell of a boat would soon be swamped by the waves!'

Karen also looked out of the window and noticed for the first time since she had woken up that the weather had changed considerably. A blustery wind was rattling at the door and was whining in the mesh of the window screens.

'I was hoping to find a fisherman to take me back in his boat,' she said. 'That's how I came here, in a fishing boat.'

'The fishermen's wharf is in Green Cove,' said Laurie. She gave Karen a bright, knowing glance. 'I could drive you over there when I've finished here and you could ask my father if he'll take you to Seaton. I'm sure he will if the weather isn't too rough.'

'Thanks. I'd be very grateful if he would take

me, and I'd pay him, of course,' said Karen. 'How much longer do you think you'll be here?'

'While the pies are baking I'll make the beds and dust upstairs. I should be through in half an hour.'

'Then I'll go and look for Tony and see you here in the kitchen in thirty minutes,' replied Karen, and walked over to the back door and into the porch.

As soon as she opened the porch door she learned about the wind. It snatched at her hair and blew it across her face and her skirt was flattened against her thighs. Leaves driven from trees whirled against her, stinging her legs and face. Pushing her hair back from her face and holding it down against her neck, she walked round to the front of the house, leaning against the wind all the way.

All the trees were swaying and creaking and the long grasses were flattened. Down on the shore she could hear the sea booming and crashing among the rocks. Thinking that Val and Tony might have gone down to the dock to make sure the boat was tied up securely, she went along the path to the small bay.

The water was high and surging towards the shore in rough grey waves, crested with white foam. Against the slanted red rocks of the protective reef white spray leapt upwards. Overhead the sky was a swiftly moving mass of clouds, some the colour of charcoal, some pearl grey and others a pale watery yellow. Under the onslaught of water and wind the timbers of the dock groaned and squealed as if in agony, and the small motorboat tugged frantically at the ropes which held it as it tried to dance away on the waves.

Neither Val nor Tony were on the dock or the

beach, so she turned back along the path. Where
had they gone? It would just be like Val to have
hidden Tony somewhere so that she couldn't persuade the boy to go with her. Not that she would
be returning to Seaton yet, she thought ruefully,
still holding her hair down as she turned to look at
the sea again. The wind was far too strong for any
small fishing boat.

She walked on, drawn by a throbbing noise to a
shed not far from the house. She opened the door
and looked inside. An electricity generator took up
most of the space. Stepping into the shed, she
walked round the generator, carefully looking into
every corner for Tony and calling his name. He
didn't appear, so she went outside and closed the
door.

Behind the shed and the house the trees were thick
and the undergrowth impenetrable. In front of the
house the land sloped away to a rocky shore. To
the left of the house a dirt road disappeared around
an outcrop of rock. It was presumably the road to
Green Cove and a blue Ford pick-up truck was
parked on it.

Val and Tony could have gone in any one of
three directions, into the wood, along the shore or
along the road. Which way should she go to look
for them? A wild gust of wind snatched at her hair
and clothing, almost making her stagger. Its coldness bit through the thin material of her clothing.
Turning, she ran round the house to the back porch
and let herself into the kitchen, thankful to be back
in shelter.

The smell of baking reminded her that she hadn't

eaten since breakfast at Milworth, so she looked into the fridge for something to eat. She was sitting at the kitchen table eating toasted cheese sandwiches and drinking milk when Laurie came into the kitchen.

'It's blowing up quite a storm out there,' Laurie said. 'I guess you won't be going to Seaton today. None of the fishermen will want to put to sea in this and any that are caught out there will be racing for shelter.'

'I don't blame them,' said Karen with a shudder. 'How long do you think the storm will last?'

'Forecast says that the wind won't abate until tomorrow afternoon,' drawled Laurie as she lifted pies from the oven. 'Could be you and Tony will be stuck here till Monday morning.' She gave Karen a sidelong glance. 'I guess that won't please you.'

'No, it doesn't please me,' sighed Karen, looking out of the window at the tumbling grey clouds.

Laurie took the last pie from the oven and closed the door. The pastry was golden-brown and some purple juice ran out of the side of the pie. All the pies looked better than any she had ever baked, thought Karen, and her glance wandered back to Laurie.

Her fair skin glowing with health, Laurie was full-breasted and strong-looking, designed to be the breeder of children, sexy in a thoroughly innocent, countrified way, and she had kept house for Val all summer, had been in this house with him every day. They hit it off together, she had said. Karen felt a sudden sharp twist of jealousy and looked away out of the window again as she wondered whether Laurie and Val had made love together. In this lonely house far away from curious eyes they had had plenty of opportunity.

The back door opened suddenly and Val came in. His hair was wind-tangled and his cheeks were red from the sting of the wind. He slammed the door closed and leaned against it, his observant eyes flicking from Karen to Laurie and back to Karen.

'Has Tony come in?' he asked.

'No.' Karen stood up quickly. 'I thought you'd gone out to find him. Wasn't he near the house when you went out?'

He shook his head from side to side.

'There was no sign of him. I went down to the beach, but he wasn't there either, so I walked part way along the road to Green Cove. Again there was no sign of him, so I came back thinking he'd been driven inside by the coldness of the wind.' He pushed away from the door and came over to Karen, to glare down at her, his mouth twisting with exasperation. 'This is all your fault! If you hadn't said you'd come to take him back to Canada he wouldn't have rushed out the way he did. God knows where he is now.'

'It's more your fault than mine,' she retorted, worry about Tony making her anger flare up. 'If you'd let me follow him when I wanted to I could have stopped him from going out. And if you hadn't kidnapped him in the first place he wouldn't have come here and I wouldn't have come for him, and he wouldn't be lost.'

'Right—shove the blame on to me.' His lips

thinned and curved back from his teeth in a bitter grimace. 'It's my fault he exists at all, is the next line. My fault because I asked you to live with me in London. *God*.' He raked a hand though his hair making it even more tousled. 'Didn't it ever occur to you that you could have refused?'

'Yes, it did many times, but. . . .' She broke off, suddenly aware that Laurie was standing there watching and listening avidly to everything, her blue eyes so wide open that the white showed all around the irises. Exerting all her self-control, Karen made herself speak more calmly. 'Is there anywhere Tony could have hidden that you know of? Any other way he could have gone?' she asked, looking pleadingly at Val.

'He could have gone along the shore over the rocks. Or he could have wandered off into the woods,' Val replied, also making an effort to be calm and matter-of-fact. He zipped up the down-filled nylon parka he was wearing over his checked shirt. 'I'll go out and look for him again.' He looked at Laurie. 'Will you look out for him on your way back to Green Cove?'

'Sure I will,' said Laurie, who was pulling on a thick black and red checked man's shirt over her cotton shirt. 'Are you coming with me, Karen?'

'Why would you want to go with Laurie?' Val demanded, swinging round to face Karen and giving her a coldly glittering glance.

'Laurie offered to take me to the village to ask her father if he would take Tony and me to Seaton,' she explained.

'Murray wouldn't go in a storm like this,' he said,

still staring at her. 'You'll have to stay the night here.'

'I'm beginning to realise that.' Karen turned and smiled at Laurie. 'I can't go with you. I'll have to wait here until Tony is found. Could you come over tomorrow to get us if the weather is better?'

'Sure thing,' Laurie nodded. 'I'll be glad to do that, and if I see Tony along the road I'll come right back with him. See you!'

She went out and Val closed the door after her. In the silent rapidly darkening kitchen he stared at Karen again as they listened to the pick-up's engine roar into life.

'I'll come with you, help you look for Tony,' Karen whispered, trying hard to keep panic at bay.

'In those shoes?' he scoffed, his glance going to her feet in their high-heeled sandals. Slowly his glance drifted upwards. 'And in that outfit?' he added softly. 'No, you stay here in case he comes back while I'm gone.'

'Supposing, supposing. . . .' Her voice choked in her throat and she covered her face with her hands as her anxiety got the better of her.

First his hands touched her shoulders gently, then somehow his arms were around her, comforting her in a familiar embrace. His long fingers stroked through her hair and then trailed down her cheek to her chin and lifted it. Against her lips his were cold and rough from the wind. They tasted and smelt salty from sea-spray, but their touch was sweetly seductive, drawing from her a response she hadn't experienced for years and had had no intention of giving. Her lips parted, her eyes closed and her body arched against his, and for a few moments they were the lovers who had met and had loved in London, giving freely of themselves to each other.

Slowly Val lifted his lips from hers and again in the silent room they studied each other.

'I'll find him, Karen, I promise,' he murmured. 'Even if it takes me all night, I'll bring him back to you.'

'I hope so. I hope so,' was all she could say.

He stepped away from her and snapped on the light switch so that yellow light flooded the room.

'It would be a good plan to put on all the lights so that he can see the house if he's in the woods,' he said matter-of-factly, looking back at her from the doorway. 'You'll be okay?'

'Yes.' She managed a rather thin smile. 'I'll wait here until you both come back.'

Val gave her one of his intent underbrowed burning glances which made her nerves quiver and expand sensuously, then opened the door and went out.

CHAPTER FOUR

KAREN had never been very good at waiting. Her imagination was too vivid and she had a tendency to envisage all sorts of catastrophes. Only in activity could she avoid imagining that Tony had fallen in the sea and drowned; or he was lost in the woods and crying because he couldn't find his way out of them. Following Val's instructions, she hurried through the house switching on all the lights, pausing at each window to look out at the swiftly-darkening windswept sky, at the heaving crested sea and at the swaying, creaking trees.

Returning to the kitchen, she decided to prepare a meal for Val and Tony. They would both want something to eat when they came in and it would keep her busy. Think positively, act positively, that was the only way to keep imaginary demons at bay. In the fridge she found a packet of minced beef and soon she was chopping onions, adding them to the beef and shaping it into hamburgers ready for cooking. Next she made a salad, pulling apart an iceberg lettuce, slicing home-grown cucumbers and tomatoes into a wooden bowl and tossing them all together. When that was done she stood in the middle of the room listening to the wind screeching and whining, wishing she could hear the noise of the pick-up Laurie had been driving as it returned, hoping that Laurie would come into the house with Tony.

Trying to blot out the sound of the wind, she turned on the transisitor radio, but reception was poor, so she turned it off and went through to the study where she had noticed a record player. On the shelves under the player records were stacked. Sifting through them, she found that Val's taste in music was as eclectic as ever, ranging from Baroque music by Telemann played on ancient instruments right through to the latest album by the Rolling Stones. She found a record of Strauss waltzes and placed it on the turn table, deciding that the lively romantic tunes were just what she needed to hear at that time of anxiety.

At the desk she sat in the swivel chair. There was a sheet of yellow paper in the typewriter. Val was obviously in the middle of writing a new novel, because the words Chapter Three were typed at the top of the page. Nothing had been typed beneath the heading and she could only assume he had been interrupted, possibly by Tony. Beside the typewriter was a pile of yellow typewritten sheets, the untyped side of the pages uppermost. Lifting the pile up she discovered, as she expected, Chapter One and Chapter Two.

She knew from the time she had lived with him that Val composed directly on the typewriter, letting his imagination flow, getting the whole story down from beginning to end almost without stopping. Only when he had finished it would he go back to the beginning again and rewrite, developing characters more deeply, revising descriptions and dialogue, creating hair-raising suspense as only he knew how. After that would come the correcting of spelling and punctuation, the drudgery, as he had often called it, of making the final typescript presentable before submitting it to a publisher.

Karen was glad he had been successful, glad that someone had recognised his great talent for telling a story. But success had changed him; she had noticed that the last time she had met him. He wasn't the young man she had known in London and was no longer preoccupied with his ambition to be a best-selling author. He had matured and, he had told her, he had found out that there was no such thing as free love after all.

How had he found out? How had he learned that lesson? Had he loved a woman and lost her as she had loved him and lost him seven years ago? Oh, how she had loved him! She had loved him so much she hadn't been able to hold on to him or make demands on him, because that hadn't been the arrangement between them, and she had believed that if she had insisted that he married her just because she had been going to have his child what little love he had had for her would have turned to hate and resentment.

Impatiently Karen pushed away from the desk. Wind buffeted the window and she went over to it to look out. Now it was so dark she couldn't see the land sloping down to the rocky shore. How could Val possibly find Tony in this murk? Which way had he gone along the shore? If he slipped and fell into the raging sea he wouldn't stand a chance.

The water would take hold of his body and dash it against the rocks. Her clenched hands pressed against her mouth. Oh, God, she must stop thinking like that. She wouldn't be able to bear it if both Tony and Val were drowned. She would die too.

Turning on her heel, she hurried back to the kitchen, pretending to herself that they would both walk into the house in a few minutes demanding a meal. She put the hamburgers in a frying pan and placed the pan on a low heat on the stove. From the fridge she took hamburger buns and put them in the oven to warm up. She was in the process of setting the kitchen table for three when she heard a thumping on the porch door and Val's voice calling to her to open the door.

She ran out into the porch. The door swung back. Light from the outside overhead lamp streamed down on Val's windblown hair. He was holding Tony in his arms, a white-faced Tony whose head lolled inertly against Val's chest and whose eyes were closed.

'Oh, where did you find him?' she gasped, standing back so that Val could enter the porch.

'On the shore. He'd fallen between two big rocks and was trapped between them. I guessed he slipped on some seaweed and banged his head. If he hadn't been howling so loudly I might never have found him,' he replied as he walked past her into the kitchen. 'I'll take him right up to bed. He's suffering from shock and exhaustion and needs to be kept warm.'

In the bedroom where she had slept that afternoon Karen watched Val lay Tony on the bed. The boy's shoes and clothing were sodden and he wasn't just pale, he was nearly blue with cold.

'I've checked his limbs to make sure he hasn't broken any of them and they seem all right, but perhaps you'd like to check too,' said Val, unzipping his parka. His cheeks were pinched with cold too and his eyes looked strained with anxiety. 'And since he banged his head he could be suffering from slight concussion.'

'Then we must take him to a doctor immediately,' said Karen firmly.

'We can't,' he retorted wearily. 'Because there is no doctor on the island, and there's no way we can go to Seaton in this storm. We'll take him to the hospital in Seaton as soon as the storm lets up. Meanwhile we'll just wrap him up, keep him warm and hope that'll he'll sleep through the night.'

'But if he's concussed he could be bleeding inside his head and develop compression of the brain,' exclaimed Karen anxiously, bending over Tony and feeling the back of his head. There was a bump there, but it wasn't very big.

'I said *slightly* concussed,' drawled Val. 'If he'd been badly concussed he wouldn't have been conscious and lucid enough to cry when he found he was stuck between the two rocks. He'd be unconscious now, but he isn't. He's wide awake.' He grinned at Tony, who had opened his eyes. 'See where you are, son? Safe in bed. Would you like something to eat?'

Tony nodded. Colour was stealing back into his cheeks.

'I'd like some milk and some cookies, please,' he said.

'Then I'll go and get them for you while your mummy undresses you,' said Val, and left the room.

'My head hurts,' moaned Tony as he sat up. 'I fell and banged it, Mummy.'

'I know you did, darling,' said Karen as she eased his shoes and socks off. 'But it will be better soon. Do you think you could sit up so that I can take your sweater and shirt off?'

He sat up, but stared at her warily from under his eyebrows, looking so much like Val that her heart seemed to shake within her breast.

'I'm not going home with you,' he said. 'I'm going to stay here with Val.'

'All right,' she replied soothingly, lifting the sweater over his head. 'We'll both stay here tonight, but tomorrow I'll have to take you to see a doctor, have him look at your head. Oh, Tony, why did you run away like that?'

'I don't want to go back home with you. I want to stay here with Val,' he muttered, glowering at her. 'Mummy, is he really my daddy?'

The grey eyes were wide open and watching her, so there wasn't much chance of her lying to him.

'Yes, he's your father,' she said shortly, easing his pants off.

'Then why don't you and I live with him all the time like other boys and mummies live with their daddies? And why has he been away from us all the time?'

'Because . . . because he didn't know about you.'

'Oh.' Tony frowned in puzzlement and scratched the skin on his chest. 'I'd like to put my pyjamas on.'

'But you don't have any here.'

'Yes, I do. They're under the pillow.' He pulled back the bedcovers and began to feel under the pillow. With an air of triumph he pulled out a pair of flannel pyjamas decorated with printed rabbits. 'Val bought them for me last night at a shopping mall.'

She helped him put them on, then escorted him to the bathroom. By the time they returned to the bedroom Val was there with a plate of cookies and a glass of milk.

'How do you feel now, Tony?' he asked, as the boy scrambled up on to the bed and slid under the blankets. 'Warmer?'

'Yes.' Tony smiled at him. 'But my head still hurts.'

'Then you'd best lie down and go to sleep,' said Val crisply. 'After you've had the cookies and milk, of course. I'll see you tomorrow. Goodnight.'

' 'Night, Daddy,' Tony muttered, his mouth full of chocolate chip cookie.

Val left the room again. Tony ate all the cookies and drank all the milk. Karen persuaded him to leave the bed again to go to the bathroom to clean his teeth, then saw him back into the bed. Not having a book to read to him, she made up a story and told it to him until at last his eyelids drooped and he slept.

For a while she sat there listening to him breathing, then, satisfied that he was sleeping properly and not in any sort of concussion-induced coma, she turned the bedside lamp low and left the room.

In the kitchen Val was sitting at the table reading a book and eating a wedge of blueberry pie. He looked up when Karen entered.

'Is he asleep?' he asked.

'Yes. Did you see the hamburgers?'

'Uhuh, I left one for you.' A slight grin crooked his mouth. 'My efforts to find Tony made my hungry so I ate two.'

She scooped up the remaining hamburger, placed it in a bun and put it on a plate which she carried over to the table. After helping herself to salad she ate in silence while Val continued to read. The wind was still whistling around the house and occasionally flurries of rain pinged against the window. In contrast to the wild storminess without the atmosphere in the kitchen was warm, glowing with golden light.

'Thank you for looking for Tony, for finding him and bringing him back,' Karen said at last.

Val looked up from his book and straight at her.

'You're welcome,' he drawled, and began to cut another wedge of the blueberry pie. 'Laurie is a good cook,' he said, quite unnecessarily, Karen thought with a little spurt of jealousy of the absent Laurie.

'She seems very domesticated,' she said stiffly. 'She would make a good wife. Why don't you marry her?'

This time his eyelids flicked up swiftly and the glance he gave her was bright with mockery.

'Maybe I will if you insist on marrying Paul

Dutton,' he retorted. 'Then Tony would have a stepmother as well as a stepfather. Would you be agreeable to having Tony looked after by Laurie?'

'No, I wouldn't,' she flared. 'Why should I? If I'd wanted him to have a mother other than myself I'd have put him up for adoption when he was born. Anyway, Laurie isn't going to have the chance of looking after him or being his stepmother. He isn't going to stay with you. I'm taking him back with me to Canada, tomorrow.'

'No, you're not,' he retorted, his face hardening. 'Tony isn't leaving this island with you to go anywhere until you've given up the idea of marrying Paul Dutton.'

'But that's blackmail!' she said accusingly. 'It means you're holding Tony hostage until I give in to your demands.'

'That's right,' he replied coolly. 'He'll only be released when you pay the ransom.'

'What ransom?'

'Marriage to me.'

'Oh, now you're behaving crazily!' she spluttered. 'Like . . . like someone in one of your stories!'

'I'm behaving like a normal man. I've just found out that I have a son and that his mother is threatening to give that son a stepfather without giving me the opportunity of being his father,' he retorted through tight lips. 'If that's behaving crazily then most of human behaviour is crazy. I want Tony to know what it's like to have a real father who cares about him.'

'Would you feel the same if Tony was a girl?' she challenged him.

'Yes, I would. Perhaps more so. Who knows?' His mouth curled sardonically. 'Maybe I'll never be allowed to find out if you refuse to marry me.'

'You ... you'd want to ... to have another child?' she whispered.

'Of course I would, once I'm married to you.'

'But even if I did give in and agreed to marry you I couldn't possibly live here,' she argued.

'Why couldn't you?'

'It's so far away from anywhere, so remote. Tony has to go to school.'

'He can go to school at Green Cove. All the fishermen's children go to school there until they're old enough to go to high school. When Tony reaches that stage we can move to the mainland, buy a house in the town so that he can still live with us while he's getting his secondary education.'

'But I couldn't possibly live here!' she repeated loudly, her voice ringing through the room. 'I have to go to work. I have a good job, a career to follow. I couldn't do it living here.'

'Once you'd married me you would give up your career,' Val replied coolly. 'There would be no need for you to go to work. I make enough money in royalties to support both of us and a family.'

'That isn't the point,' Karen retorted, angered by his arrogant assumptions. 'I like my work. I enjoy it.'

'But wouldn't you enjoy being at home looking after your family more?' he argued softly. He looked across at her his eyes warm with sympathy. 'It must have been hell for you, Karen, having to leave Tony with someone else when he was a baby so that you could go to work. Think of the hours of his company you've missed while he's been developing; the best times in a child's life.' His face hardened again. 'You've wilfully deprived me of those times with my own child too, that's why I've taken him away from you. Why I'm going to keep him here, to live with me. But unlike you I'm willing to share him with you if you'll agree to marry me.' He leaned towards her, his eyes ablaze with the intensity of his feelings, and again she felt her nerves quiver in response to that look. 'We could share in Tony's upbringing, we could share everything, Karen, like we used to when we lived together in London. Remember the good times we had together? We could have them again.'

Her heart seemed to lurch against her ribs. She knew only too well what he meant when he referred to the good times. He meant the times they had made love together, when he had taken her by the hand and had led her along the path of sensuous pleasure, teaching her to arouse his passion while he had aroused in her a powerful, overwhelming desire to be a part of him so that she had succumbed willingly to his possession of her body, believing that by doing so he would become a part of her and that eventually she would possess him completely. But it hadn't worked out that way. In the end he had avoided being possessed and had let her leave him. He had let her leave him and had made no attempt to follow her, to win her back, and for that she had great difficulty in forgiving him.

'No.' She shook her head, shaking away the disturbing memories of the joyous ecstasy they had once experienced together. 'We can never have those times again. Never.'

'Why can't we?'

'Because . . . oh, because I'm different now from what I was then. I'm not a curious, naïve young woman any more. I'm an adult person with some experience of life. I need more from a relationship than just sexual gratification,' she replied coolly.

'We had more than sexual gratification going for us in our relationship and you know it,' Val growled at her, his eyes glinting at her angrily. 'We communicated on more than one level.'

'You didn't love me,' she said, looking at him steadily.

'I came as close to loving you as I ever have to loving anyone,' he grated between thinning lips. 'That was why I let you keep your freedom.'

'I don't believe you. I don't believe you,' Karen muttered, clutching her suddenly hot cheeks between her hands and staring down at her plate. 'Oh, please, forget those times we had together, Val. I have.'

Pushing away from the table, he stood up. She could almost feel the anger which was throbbing through him.

'Okay, I will,' he said. 'We'll start from scratch, as if we hadn't met before.' He turned away. 'I have work to do and I'll be writing till the early hours of the morning,' he added stiffly. 'Make yourself at home and when you want to go to bed feel free to use the bed in the front room. I'll sleep downstairs.'

The stingingly cold politeness of his attitude helped to stiffen her pride. Her head went up and she gave him a disdainful glance.

'I'll sleep with Tony, thank you.'

'That bed is too narrow for both of you.'

'We've slept together in a small bed before,' she retorted.

'Please yourself.' Val shrugged his shoulders as he turned away and walked towards the study.

He shut the study door behind him, not with a slam but with a loud click as if to indicate that she wouldn't be welcome in that room. Alone, Karen sagged, all the pride going out of her. Elbows on the table, she cupped her face in her hands, feeling tears prick her eyes. Why had it hurt so much to hurt him? Why had she said she had forgotten those good times they had had together in London? What was the matter with her? Why did her feelings keep see-sawing wildly between pride and passion? Surely she wasn't falling in love with him all over again? Oh, no, she mustn't let that happen. She'd suffered enough from being in love with him. It had taken her years to get over it; seven long years of hard work, of changing herself from a sensitive, wide-eyed, freely-loving girl, into the posed career woman fully in control of her own life and her child's.

Sniffing, she wiped the tears from her eyes and picked up the pie slice. Purple juice, thick with blueberries, oozed out as she cut a wedge and transferred it to her plate. The golden-brown pastry was as light as a feather, breaking up into tiny flakes as he cut into the wedge with her fork. The first morsel was delicious, melting in the mouth and titillating the appetite. As she ate the last few crumbs she had to admit reluctantly that Laurie was an excellent cook.

She cleared the table and washed the dishes. Then remembering the state of Tony's clothes she went upstairs and collected them. Returning to the kitchen, she pulled out the small portable washing machine that she had noticed, attached the hose to the single mixer tap in the sink and pushed the plug into a convenient electric socket.

When the clothes were washed and spun dry she hung them on a rack over the wood stove to finish drying, cleaned out the washing machine and returned it to its corner. Since there was nothing else for her to do in the kitchen she went through the dining room intending to go upstairs again and go to bed, as shortage of sleep the previous night plus the anxiety she had experienced waiting for Tony, to say nothing of the efforts involved in sparring with Val, had taken a toll of her nervous energy. She felt exhausted.

In the hallway she hesitated, drawn to the archway that led into the study by the tap-tap-tap of the typewriter and the sound of music coming from the record player. Only two lights were on in the room, a standard studio lamp which slanted light over Val's left shoulder on to the typewriter and a desk lamp. The rest of the room was in shadow.

As she watched quietly from the doorway Val stopped typing, leaned forward and removed the page he had typed from the machine. Lounging back in the swivel chair, he lifted his long legs and put his feet on the corner of the desk, then began to read what he had typed.

There were some things which hadn't changed. While he continued to write for his living there would always be evenings like this when he would go off into a world of his own; a world Karen couldn't enter and wouldn't know about until the story was published and she could read it. She could go into the room now, sit in a chair, read a book and listen to the music and he would never know she was there. He didn't need her. He had never needed her except in one way, as a woman who could satisfy his sexual desires, and there were probably other women who could have done that seven years ago and had done it since she and he had been apart. Probably Laurie had done it, here in this house.

Karen gagged suddenly as jealousy of Laurie curdled within her, and she stepped back from the doorway quickly and went upstairs determined not to repeat history, refusing to enter the room where Val was working to wait for him to stop writing and turn to her to lift her to her feet and take her in his arms. Those times were over and done with. They were starting from scratch as if nothing had ever happened between them; as if they were strangers.

Tony was still fast asleep, his slight form moulded by the blankets that covered him, his hair black as pitch against the pillow. Looking down at him, Karen felt once again that violent swing in her emotions. How could she or Val pretend they had never been together? Tony was here with them, the lovely evidence and product of their passionate desire for each other when they had lived together in London. He was their love-child.

She prepared for bed, undressing in the bathroom and washing, shivering a little as cool air touched her skin, then slipped into the pale blue nightgown of sheer blue nylon chiffon which clung to her breasts and shaped her thighs, wishing she had brought something warmer and less attractive to wear at night. There wasn't much room for her to lie beside Tony because he was sleeping right in the middle of the bed, but she managed to slide under the blankets without disturbing him. She settled her head on the corner of the only pillow, switched out the bedside lamp and closed her eyes.

Tomorrow she would have a long talk with Val, a sensible discussion. He must be made to see that she had come to get Tony back and not to be with him, not to rekindle their affair, not to. . . . Sleep overcame her suddenly.

For a few hours she was oblivious to time and place, but after a while she found herself lying on the edge of a steep cliff looking down at a rocky shore far below where the sea crashed, sending up huge plumes of feathery spray. Suddenly she seemed to be rolling off the cliff. She screamed for help. Over the edge she fell downwards to the jagged sea-swept rocks, crying out in her terror, shouting for Val to come and help her. She fell with a bump and almost immediately was swept up again by strong arms.

She woke with a start and opened her eyes to

darkness save where faint, intermittent moonlight breaking through clouds trickled into the room through the window. Remembering where she was, glad to find she hadn't really rolled over the edge of a cliff, Karen reached out an arm to feel for Tony. He wasn't there!

Frantically she groped and her fingers touched, instead of a thin flannel-covered childish body, the crisp hairs on a man's hard chest. She snatched her hand back, thinking she was dreaming again, and blinked her eyes rapidly, trying to see in the darkness.

The window was in the wrong place. In the room where Tony slept the window was in a wall beside the bed. Now it was in a wall at the foot of the bed. She must be in the other bed, the big double bed. Then how had she got there? Had she walked in her sleep? She reached out again. This time her fingertips touched a hairy forearm that tensed slightly under her touch.

'Val?'

'Uhuh?'

So he was lying beside her in the bed and she hadn't imagined he was there.

'How did I get here?'

'I carried you in.'

'Why?'

'I was just getting ready for bed when you screamed. I went to see what was wrong in time to see you fall out of the other bed. You were very cold in that flimsy gown you're wearing, so I brought you in here and put you in this bed. I'd just got into bed when you woke up.'

'You shouldn't have brought me in here. I don't want to sleep with you. That isn't why I came here,' she retorted.

'Isn't it?' he mocked.

'Of course it isn't. I came to get Tony and I'm not leaving the island until I can take him with me.'

'Good,' he murmured, aggravatingly agreeable. He shifted across the space that separated them, put an arm about her waist and began to draw her backwards against the curve of his warm body.

'No, please don't do that,' she protested, her hand on his trying to pull it away from her waist. 'I'm not staying in this bed. I'm going back to the other room. I don't want to be held by you. I don't want you to touch me!'

'Afraid?' Val jeered. His head was close to hers and she felt his breath tickle the delicate skin of her earlobe. 'Don't be. I'm only going to hold you until you're warm again, until you fall asleep.' He yawned softly and added sleepily, 'It's almost three in the morning and I'm pretty tired. So relax, sweetheart. Sleep while you can. If his behaviour this morning is anything to go by Tony is going to be waking up in about three hours' time and then there'll be no more sleep for either of us.'

Warmth radiating out from his body crept through her slowly. Her toes curled instinctively in the direction of his hard shins and rubbed against his skin so that he gasped with shock at their icy touch.

In the dark silence she could hear their heart-beats. Hers was too fast, betraying her tension and excitement at finding herself in close proximity to Val's hard pulsing body. His was strong and steady, somehow expressive of his determination to get what he wanted, to take over the running of Tony's life.

He moved against her, nuzzling the thick hair at her neck, pushing it aside with the tip of his nose. Against the sensitive skin of her nape his lips were warm and then the tip of his tongue was hard and hot, as it licked and tickled until shivers ran down her spine and tingles of desire danced along her nerves.

'You taste good and you smell good,' he whispered. 'You feel good too.' His hand moved up from her waist to her breast, which was already tautening in anticipation of his touch. 'I'm glad you've decided to stay for a while on the island.'

'I didn't say I'd decided to stay,' Karen argued, her fingers pulling vainly at his trying to remove them from her breast, while a longing to turn to him and press her hungry body all along the length of his in invitation swept through her weakening her resistance. 'All I said was I'm not leaving until I can take him with me, until he agrees to go back to Canada with me. You must see that you can't keep him here. He has no legal status here.'

'To hell with legal status,' he murmured, sliding his hand within the deep V of the bodice of her nightgown so that it was her turn to gasp as his fingertips pinched soft flesh. 'He's mine, my natural son and heir.' His lips tantalised the curve of her neck and she stifled a groan, wondering vaguely how she had managed to sleep alone for so long without the sweet torment of his fingers touching her skin, without the fire of his kisses to inflame her senses. Seven long years without him sharing her bed until now; without any man sharing her bed; seven long years of abstinence. How had she done it? Why had she done it? And why should she abstain now when Val was there behind her?

She half turned within the circle of his arm so that she was lying on her back and waited for him to make his move, expecting him to raise himself up, then lower his lips to hers, to slide across her in subtle domination of her body with his. Excitement rippled through her in anticipation of feeling his urgent demands, knowing he would quench the thirst of her desire and release her from the agony of tension.

'Val,' she whispered. 'I'm only going to stay until tomorrow. I have to go back tomorrow. I can't stay here and I can't leave Tony with you. Please try to understand. We can't stay with you.'

He didn't speak and his hand had gone slack, sliding away from her breast. She turned towards him urgently, her fingers seeking his chest, sliding up to his throat.

'Val!'

He didn't answer. Her fingers trailed upwards over his bristly chin, flitted tentatively over the curve of his lips, traced the straight line of his nose and touched one eye socket, finding the lashes lying thickly against the skin, the eyelid closed over the eye. He was breathing quietly and regularly. He was asleep.

Disappointment was a sharp knife stabbing her

heart and frustration was a raw ache at the pit of her stomach. He had fallen asleep as swiftly as Tony often fell asleep and there wasn't going to be any lovemaking after all, no attempt on his part to continue to rouse her desires so that he could · satisfy his own.

She was free now to leave the bed if she wanted to go back to the other room, but she didn't go. Biting back the groans of disappointment and pique, clenching her hands so that they wouldn't reach out to pinch and pummel him until he woke up, Karen turned on to her side again and, settling her body into the curve of his, took his slack hand and arm and drew them across her waist again, holding them in place to comfort her until she went to sleep again.

When she awoke again the ceiling was dappled with yellow sunlight and the moving shadows of leaves and branches. She stared at the flickering shadows for a moment in puzzlement, then looked towards the window at the fluttering red leaves of a big maple tree growing close to the house. Through the leaves she could see patches of blue sky and fluffy white clouds. Although the wind was still whistling about the house it looked as if the worst of the storm was over.

She was alone in the bed and the house was very quiet. Too quiet. It was strange not to hear Tony singing to himself as he usually did when he woke up in the morning. Perhaps he didn't feel well. Perhaps he hadn't woken up. Suddenly anxious, she pushed aside the bedclothes and left the bed, padding along to the other bedroom on bare feet.

The door of the other room was wide open and the bed was empty. Tony had gone. Downstairs she went in a rush, sure that she would find Tony with Val in the kitchen. On the table two cereal bowls, both empty, yet still containing a few soggy cornflakes and two glasses containing the dregs of orange juice, seemed to mock her. In the middle of the table was a piece of yellow copy paper. She snatched the paper up and read the words Val had scrawled on it: *Tony and I have gone fishing. See you later.*

How dared he! How dared he take Tony out with him before she was awake, before she had seen the child and had made sure he was fit to go fishing, before she had had time to check if his clothing was dry enough to put on? Just who did Val think he was, taking over her child like that? *He's Tony's father. Tony's father.* The words whispered through her mind repeatedly.

Her fingers curled around the piece of paper, crumpling it into a ball, and in sudden irritation she threw it across the room as hard as she could. Feeling better for that little display of temper, she turned to leave the room and caught sight of the rack over the wood stove, and her eyes widened. Tony's clothes were still there. Then what was he wearing? Surely he hadn't gone fishing in his pyjamas?

Gone fishing. Where? On the sea. Going through to the dining room, she looked out of the window down the slope of land. The sea was a glittering blue crested with white, not as wild as it had been the previous evening but still too rough for Val's

small motorboat. Had he and Tony gone in one of
the big fishing boats? Had Laurie come over and
taken them to Green Cove with her so they could
go out with her father? Was Laurie with them on
the trip, standing beside Val, almost as tall as he
was, smiling at him adoring him with her big blue
eyes as she slid an arm through his? *Grrr!* Karen
growled in her throat and ground her teeth.

Val should have wakened her, and told her what
he had planned. He should have given her a chance
to refuse to let Tony go fishing with him. Or he
should have given her a chance to go too. Oh, if
she lived with him it would be like this all the time,
if she agreed to do what he wanted and married
him. Always a law to himself, he would do what
he wanted without ever consulting her. He would
organise and rule Tony's life and she would lose
the child to him just as surely as she would lose
Tony if she left and went back to Canada today
without him.

She glanced up at the old-fashioned wall clock,
its pendulum swinging from side to side within a
glass-fronted case, and received another shock. It
was almost noon. She had slept very late. A
throbbing noise drew her attention back to the
window. The blue pick-up truck had appeared
round the outcrop of rock and was stopping where
the rough road ended. Had Tony and Val returned,
driven by Laurie?

Both doors of the truck swung open and from
the driver's side Laurie emerged, her smooth
blonde hair glinting in the sunlight. She was
dressed in the same jeans, shirt and man's thick

black and red shirt she had worn the day before. Karen looked away from her to the person who was slamming closed the door on the other side of the truck, and received her third surprise of the morning.

Wearing a heavy hooded parka over his suit, his brown hair slightly dishevelled by the wind, Paul Dutton turned away from the truck and, briefcase in hand, followed Laurie across the grass towards the house.

CHAPTER FIVE

Quickly Karen backed away from the dining room window and hurried into the hall. Up the stairs she bounded two at a time and went into Tony's room. Flinging off her nightgown, she dressed in a crisp cotton blouse, a pair of slacks tailored in fine black wool, and a V-necked sweater knitted in thick bubbly lilac-coloured bouclé wool. She strapped on her high-heeled sandals, gave her hair a quick brush, outlined her lips in a dark red lipstick, then went downstairs again and into the kitchen.

Laurie was just closing the door and Paul was standing in the middle of the room looking about him. In his city business suit with his briefcase dangling from his hand he looked out of place in the homely kitchen of the old country house. As soon as he saw Karen he stepped across to her.

'Paul, how did you get here?' she exclaimed, holding up both hands to keep him away from her as he leaned forward as if to kiss her.

'I flew to Bangor yesterday and I would have come over to the island yesterday afternoon if the storm hadn't blown up. I came over as soon as I could this morning to Green Cove. Miss Arnold,' he gestured towards Laurie, 'kindly offered to drive me here.' He looked up at the big beams that crossed the ceiling and then round at the wide horizontal planks of pinewood of the walls. 'This house must be quite old,' he remarked.

'Nearly a hundred and fifty years old,' said Laurie, taking off her red and black shirt and hanging it behind the kitchen door. 'It was built by one of the first settlers on the island. His name was Knight and Val believes he's descended from him.'

'But how did you find out Val lives here?' asked Karen.

'From the State police,' replied Paul, as he slipped off his parka and laid it down on a nearby chair. 'When they learned why I wanted to find him they were very quick to locate him for me.' His smile was smug.

'What did you tell them?' demanded Karen.

'That he'd kidnapped Tony, of course.' He came back to stand before her. 'All you have to do is say the word, darling, and I can have them over here to arrest him on the charge.'

'But I don't want Val arrested! I don't want the police in on this. I can handle the situation myself,' she retorted angrily, glaring up at him, little flecks of gold burning brightly in the velvet brown darkness of her eyes. 'And I told you to stay out of it, too. I can't understand why you've followed me here.'

'I came because I was worried about you, darling.' He gave the watching, listening Laurie a quick glance, then added in a lower voice, 'Is there another room where we can go to talk privately?'

'We can go into the dining room, I suppose,' said Karen reluctantly. She also glanced at Laurie. 'Tony and Val have gone fishing. Do you have any idea where?' she asked.

'I guess they've gone to Long Pond,' replied Laurie. 'It isn't far from here. Val often goes there to fish. Where did he find Tony?'

'Along the shore, somewhere. He'd fallen and had got stuck between two rocks. I was just going to make some coffee. Would you like to make it, please, and bring it into the dining room. Mr Dutton and I have some business to discuss.'

'Sure,' agreed Laurie pleasantly. 'I asked my father if he would take you back to Seaton and he says he will, any time.'

'Thanks,' said Karen. 'I'll let you know when.' She turned back to Paul. 'The dining room is this way.'

Once they were in the room she closed the door and took a chair at one end of the shining oval oak table. Paul pulled another chair out, but before he sat down, he looked round the room with a frown.

'This is a bit cold and formal,' he remarked. 'I feel as if we're going to have a board meeting. Isn't there a room where we could be more relaxed and sit together on a chesterfield?' He smiled meaningfully at her. 'I mean to say, I feel our relationship is a little closer than that of lawyer and client.'

'There's only the sitting room and Val uses that as his den or study to write in, and I don't think he would like it if I took you in there. Anyway, I feel cold and formal this morning. You had no right to come here, Paul.'

'I've told you I was worried about you,' he returned smoothly as he sat down. He put his elbows on the table and linking his fingers rested his chin on them. His glasses made him look like an owl, Karen thought, a myopic and not very young owl.

'Why were you worried?' she asked.

'I had a feeling you might be trapped into staying in Knight's house,' he replied. 'You stayed the night here with him, didn't you?'

'Yes, I did. I couldn't do anything else because of the storm. It was the wind that trapped me here, not Val,' she replied spiritedly. 'And you can be sure I wouldn't have stayed if I could have got back to Seaton with Tony, but he ran away and . . . well, I had to stay until he was found.'

'Coming here and staying here could have had dangerous consequences for you, don't you realise that, Karen?' Paul looked severe and suddenly extremely prim. 'That's why I wanted to come with you in the first place. Knight is probably very angry with you for having denied him the privilege of being a father, and he could hurt you physically.'

'Oh, no.' She shook her head from side to side so vigorously that her bright hair sparked with ruby lights in the sunlight. 'You don't know Val at all, and I do. I know he would never hit a woman. When he's angry he doesn't hit out physically. He has much more subtle ways of expressing his anger. Have you forgotten he's a writer and so has a great command of words? When he strikes out it's with words.'

'I wasn't thinking of beating or hitting,' said Paul stiffly. 'I was thinking of . . . well, to put it plainly, Karen, I was thinking he might force you to submit to him. I was thinking he might rape you.' He leaned towards her, his small brown eyes pinpointing hers. 'Has he, Karen?' he asked in a sharp voice.

'Oh, really, Paul, you do get carried away!' she replied with a little laugh. 'And the answer is no, Val hasn't raped me ever, not even when I knew him in London.' She looked at him curiously. 'You're really worried about what happened between him and me last night, aren't you?' she accused softly. 'You don't trust me.'

'That isn't the case at all,' he replied huffily, sitting back in his chair, his glance avoiding hers, dull red staining his cheeks. 'Has he told you why he kidnapped Tony and brought him here?' he asked, changing the subject quickly.

'He has. He objects to the idea of you becoming Tony's stepfather,' she said coolly, and Paul looked up sharply.

'Oh. Why is that?' he demanded.

'He doesn't want any other man being responsible for Tony's upbringing while he's still alive and he says that if I persist in marrying you and taking Tony to live with you he'll fight to get custody of the boy.'

'Really?' Paul's eyes glinted and his eyebrows went up. 'That's very interesting,' he murmured. 'And how have you reacted to that?'

'I've told him I can't agree to let him have Tony, of course. He has no legal claim to the child.'

'True,' Paul nodded. 'How did he reply to that?'

'He ... he ... well, he suggested that if I do marry you Tony will run away. He'll run to him. I said that if that happened you would find some grounds for sueing him for kidnapping Tony or something like that.'

'And what did he say to that?'

'He threatened to . . . to smirch my reputation in court to such an extent that no judge would allow me to keep Tony,' she whispered.

'I see,' said Paul. There was a short silence while he stared frowningly at the table, obviously considering what she had told him. After a while he looked at her. 'I think you should agree to let him have Tony to live with him,' he told her. 'It would be much the easiest way out of a difficult situation.'

'You mean I should give in to Val and let him have custody of Tony without a fight, in the same way you gave in to Bernice ten years ago and let her have the custody of your two daughters when she and you divorced?' Karen exclaimed. 'But I want Tony to live with me. I couldn't give him up, not after all this time. I want to be with him as much as possible. I want to be responsible for his schooling and for seeing that he grows up straight and stable,' she protested. 'I love him dearly and I want to do my best for him.'

Laurie appeared in the doorway from the kitchen with a small tray on which were two steaming mugs of coffee, a cream jug and a sugar bowl. She set the tray down on the table.

'It's just about lunchtime,' she drawled. 'Would you like me to make some sandwiches?'

'Yes, please,' said Karen. 'I haven't had breakfast yet.'

The young woman left the room and closed the door behind her. Paul drew one of the coffee mugs towards him and poured some cream into it.

'She told me on the way here that she's been housekeeping all summer for Knight,' he said, as he stirred his coffee. 'Is she his mistress?'

'I don't know,' replied Karen flatly. 'And even if she is I don't think it's any of your business.'

'You're very much on the defensive about him.'

'I'm not defending him. But I don't see that the way he chooses to live has anything to do with you. Val isn't married, so he's free to have a mistress if he wants. He doesn't have a wife to hurt in that way.'

There was another short silence during which they both sipped their coffee. Then Paul said:

'There's one thing that puzzles me about all this. Why didn't you tell me you'd met Knight again when you visited Seaton at the end of June?'

'I didn't think I was under an obligation then to tell you everything that happens to me. At that time, if you care to remember, I hadn't agreed to marry you. I'm not married to you yet, and that's why I'm resenting your interference now,' Karen retorted, her eyes sparkling dangerously again. 'You shouldn't have followed me here, and I hope you'll have the decency to leave before Val returns with Tony.'

'I'm not leaving until we've sorted this business out,' Paul replied doggedly, frowning at her. 'You know, Karen, you're far too accustomed to having your own way.'

'Well!' she gasped. 'How dare you speak to me

as if I were a naïve teenager! I'm a grown woman and I've been making decisions for myself, solving my own problems for some years. If I appear to be getting my own way all the time that's because I've managed to make the right decisions and have found successful solutions to my problems. I'm not leaving here without Tony, and so far he's refused to come with me back to the mainland.'

'Refused?' exclaimed Paul. 'My God, that little devil needs a good spanking, and he'll certainly get it if he disobeys either of us once you and I are married. Actually, it was about the matter of Tony's schooling that I wanted to talk to you this weekend while we were up at the cottage. He should go to a private boarding school. I know a good one in Ontario which takes boys in from the age of seven. Several of my colleagues have sent their sons there. The discipline is strict and the boys who attend have some sense knocked into them. If we put his name down now I'm sure they would take him in next fall and. . . .'

'We'll do nothing of the sort!' Karen interrupted him furiously, springing to her feet. 'I would rather leave Tony here with Val than . . . than send him to that sort of school!'

'All right, all right,' said Paul soothingly, also rising to his feet and walking round the table towards her. Hands on her shoulders, he turned her towards him. 'Then why don't you leave the boy here? I know he doesn't like me and heaven knows, I can't stand the sight of him.'

'Paul!' she exclaimed, in objection.

'I'm sorry, but I can't. He comes between you

and me. He makes too many demands on your time. . . .'

'He's my child!'

'And then every time I see him he reminds me that once you had an affair, a very close passionate affair with another man, and now I know that man is Knight.'

'You're jealous of Val?' she exclaimed in surprise.

'You're darned right I am!'

'But you have no reason to be. Our affair ended seven years ago. He means nothing to me now and I mean nothing to him. He wants Tony, not me.'

'Then let him have Tony. You and I would be much happier without the boy, you know. He'll always cause trouble between us. Let him stay with his father.'

And as Karen stared at him in horror at what he was suggesting he bent his head quickly and kissed her on the lips. No response flared up in her. She felt no desire to put her arms about him or to press against him. In fact she felt strangely detached, as if she were standing outside herself watching him kissing her.

'Ahem!' Laurie's cough made Paul raise his head quickly and look round.

'What do you want?' he demanded rudely.

'I've brought the sandwiches,' drawled Laurie, putting a plateful of sandwiches made from whole-wheat bread on the table. 'They're crab salad. I hope you like them. Would you like more coffee?'

'If we do we'll go into the kitchen and help ourselves,' said Paul icily.

He hadn't liked being caught kissing her by
Laurie, thought Karen. It was something that
might be used in evidence against him at some time
in the future. That was the way his mind worked
all the time, cautiously. She couldn't imagine him
ever behaving on impulse as she often did. Even
his coming here had been carefully prearranged.
He had come in the hope of doing a deal with Val
and herself, in the hope of separating her from
Tony so as to avoid trouble between himself and
her in the future. Unlike Val, who wanted only her
son, Paul wanted only her. If she married him she
would lose Tony, one way or another, either to
Val or a boarding school. So wouldn't it be best
not to marry Paul, after all?

'I'll go up and make the beds now,' Laurie said
on her way to the hallway. 'Then I'll be going back
to Green Cove, if either of you want a drive that
way. . . .'

She left the suggestion hanging in the air and
leaving the dining room clumped up the stairs.
Snatching a sandwich and cramming most of it into
her mouth, Karen followed Laurie, muttering a
vague excuse to Paul. She found the young woman
in Tony's bedroom in the act of plumping the
pillow, and closed the door.

'Laurie, I need your help,' she said breathlessly
before she could change her mind.

Laurie looked across the bed at her, her blue
eyes wide and rounded.

'How can *I* help *you?*' she asked rather sus-
piciously.

'I have to find Tony and take him back to the

mainland this afternoon without either Val or Mr Dutton knowing, and I think you'll be willing to help me because you don't want Tony and me to stay here, do you?' Karen stared challengingly at her.

'I've never said that I don't want you to stay,' replied Laurie, becoming sullen.

'I know you've never said it, but you've thought it. You're in love with Val and so you resent me because Val knew me before he knew you, because he once had an affair with me.'

'That's true,' muttered Laurie sulkily. 'You've spoilt everything since he met you again in June, since he found out you'd had his kid.'

'So you'd like me to take Tony away from here, wouldn't you?' said Karen, pressing her advantage. 'You'd like it if Val saw neither of us again.'

'I don't mind Tony so much,' said Laurie, and from under her eyebrows she gave Karen a sulky blue stare, 'but I hate you for what you've done to Val. Yes, I'd like it if he never saw you again.'

'But I can't leave without Tony, and Tony won't go with with me if he thinks I'm with Mr Dutton. Somehow I have to get Tony away from Val and into your truck so you can drive the two of us to Green Cove and your father's fishing boat. Can you think of any way we could do that?'

Laurie smoothed a sheet with one big hand, swathes of her long blonde hair falling forward along her rounded cheeks and over her shoulders and breasts.

'I could go and fetch Val and Tony from the lake,' she said slowly at last. 'I could tell them you

want to see them back at the house.' She pulled
the blanket up over the sheet and smoothed that
too. She seemed to take a sensual pleasure in
making the bed. 'When I get back here I could
stay in the truck and keep Tony with me for a
while when Val goes into the house to see you, and
you could be hiding near the generator shed ready
to get into the truck as soon as Val turns his back
on it. Then we could drive off.'

'But how will you keep Tony in the truck?' asked
Karen. 'I wouldn't like you to use physical force.'

'And I wouldn't,' retorted Laurie, her eyes flash-
ing. 'I'll think of something. I'll find something to
show him and Val will never suspect me of delaying
Tony deliberately.'

'All right,' sighed Karen, 'we'll try it. You go
now to fetch them while I pack my overnight bag.
I don't think I'll have any trouble in persuading
Mr Dutton to wait in the house to see Val.'

Laurie put the patchwork quilt on the bed and
smoothed it into place, then looked across at Karen
with her eyes glinting with something like humour.

'I guess Val is going to be pretty mad when he
finds out out how we tricked him,' she drawled.

'I guess he is,' replied Karen, feeling something
like regret stir in her because if they pulled off the
trick she wouldn't ever see Val again, and she
didn't really want him to have bad feelings about
her.

'But he'll get over it,' said Laurie with a touch
of complacency. '*I'll* see to that. I'm good at talking
him out of his bad moods.'

'Mmm, I can imagine you are,' murmured Karen

as another knife-like stab of jealousy thrust through her, thinking that Laurie who had been with Val all summer long was free to stay with him all winter long too, right into next spring and next summer, free to stay with him for the rest of her life if she wanted. 'How long do you think it will take you to pick him and Tony up and come back here?'

'About fifteen minutes, unless they've started to walk back already. You'd best leave the house ten minutes after I've gone just to be sure you're in hiding by the time I get back.'

As soon as Laurie left the room Karen changed into her tweed suit, packed her other clothing, made up her face again and brushed her hair. Then with her overnight bag slung over her shoulder she went downstairs. She left the bag on the bottom step ready for her to pick up when she left the house by way of the front door and went into the dining room. Paul was still sitting at the table eating the last sandwich. His sharp glance noted her change of clothing.

'You look as if you're all ready to leave,' he remarked.

'I am. I've sent Laurie to bring Val and Tony back from the lake. We'll talk over the idea of leaving Tony here with Val and try to come to some terms with him.'

'I'm glad you've seen the sense of my suggestion,' he said. 'The more I think about it the more it seems right to me to leave the boy here with his natural father, and Knight seems to want to take the responsibility of him. We'll insist, of course, that you must be allowed to see Tony whenever you want, have him to stay with you for holidays and so on.' Paul leaned back in the chair and stroked his chin with one hand. 'I don't recall ever having had to handle a case like this before . . . where the couple concerned weren't married . . . but there's always a first time for everything. Perhaps I should recommend to Knight that he adopt Tony as his son, that way he could give him his name.'

'Perhaps you should,' said Karen woodenly. She was beginning to wish she hadn't made the arrangement with Laurie to trick Val. She wanted to see Val again and talk to him. There was so much she hadn't told him yet about Tony, little intimate details about the boy that a mother could only share with the father of her child. There was so much too that she hadn't told him about herself and so much she wanted to know about what he had done and where he had been during the past seven years. She didn't want to leave this comfortable old house yet, but the ten minutes stipulated by Laurie was up. She rose to her feet and walked towards the hallway.

'Where are you going?' asked Paul.

'I've just remembered something I want to look at outside. I won't be long,' she said coolly.

To her relief he didn't offer to go with her. In the hall Karen picked up her overnight bag, opened the front door and stepped outside. The clear crisp air was cool against her cheeks and under her feet yellow and red leaves crunched as she walked towards the generator shed. To her right the sea sparkled blue and gold, stretching away to more islands, blobs of misty purple in the distance. To the left the woods were dark green, their gloom splintered here and there by shafts of golden light that twinkled on the yellow leaves and silver trunks of birches.

Against the side of the shed hidden from the house Karen leaned and listened for the sound of the pick-up truck coming along the road. All she heard was the throb of the generator in the shed behind her, the whistling of birds in the trees and the boom of the waves falling on the unseen shore.

It was a beautiful fall day, glittering with bright colour. She and Val had first met in this season and always the colours would be associated in her mind with loving him, with walking and talking with him as they had wandered about the London parks. This island was a park in itself, a place of peace where one could get close to nature. If she agreed to marry him he would expect her to live here with him at least for part of the year. He would expect her to give up working and stay at home, keep house, look after him and Tony, do everything a proper wife would do.

But how could she agree to marry him when she knew he only wanted to marry her to get possession of Tony and not because he loved her? On the other hand, Paul wanted to marry her but didn't want to have Tony living with him. Didn't that prove that he didn't love her either? If he loved her he would be willing to have Tony live with them all the time and wouldn't be talking about sending the child away to boarding school. If she had known that he

felt like that about Tony she would never have
agreed to marry him. She didn't love him, had
never been in love with him as she had been in love
with Val. *Then why the hell have you promised to
marry him?* Val's harshly spoken words rang
through her mind and she recalled her own wild
defensive answers, all of which had been based on
the truth. She was tired of being on her own, Tony
did need a father and she had believed until a few
moments ago that Paul loved her.

But not any more. If Paul didn't want Tony to
live with them after they were married he didn't
love her and wasn't even close to understanding
her love for her child. Why did she love Tony so
much? Why had she been so determined to keep
him once she had realised she had conceived? Why
had she struggled all these years to look after him
on her own? The answer came in a blinding flash.
She had kept him because he had been the product
of her love for Val. For her, he represented the
most wonderful year of her life, a time she had
always believed she could never have again.

From the woods came the sound of voices, the
clear piping treble of a child followed by the deeper
timbre of a man's voice answering. Surprised,
Karen looked round. Val and Tony were coming
along a narrow path which was overgrown by
bushes and tangled undergrowth. She pushed away
from the shed, looking round, wondering whether
to hide from them or not, but before she could
hide Tony had noticed her.

'Mummy, Mummy—look, look! I caught a fish.
Look, look!'

She turned towards him. He ran up to her and held out a tiny silvery trout tied to a thin line which he held in his hand. His grey eyes shone with pride and the corners of his mouth turned up at the corners in a smile of pure delight. He looked as if everything was right in his world for once.

'I caught him my own self,' he said proudly. 'Daddy didn't help me one bit.'

'Poor little fish,' murmured Karen, who wasn't thinking about the fish at all but about how easily Tony had given up calling Val by his first name and had adopted the habit of calling him Daddy since she had assured him that Val was really his father. 'He isn't very big,' she added, keeping her glance on the fish, aware that Val was now standing behind Tony and that knowledge of his presence was having the usual effect on her; her heart was beginning to beat unevenly and a thin sweat was beginning to film her skin. 'Perhaps you should have thrown him back into the lake so that he could have grown bigger.'

'You can't expect him to throw back the first fish he's ever caught,' Val rebuked her softly. 'Are you going somewhere?'

She looked up. In the bright sunlight the thick tumbled fronds of his black hair shone with golden light and under the level black eyebrows his eyes were narrowed and observant, their glance swerving from her face to the leather strap of the overnight bag over her shoulder.

'For a walk,' she lied brightly, her glance faltering away from his eyes when they looked at her again. 'To see if I could find you and Tony. I . . . I asked Laurie to look out for you along the road.'

'We came back through the woods,' he replied. 'Do you usually take your overnight bag with you when you go for a walk?'

She looked up at him again. It had always been impossible for her to lie to him, and she couldn't do it now.

'I was expecting Laurie to come back with you. I was waiting for her to come back to pick me up and drive me . . . and Tony . . . to Green Cove.' She found she was speaking hesitantly, almost stammering, because the expression in Val's eyes had changed. He was looking at her with a frank and sensual admiration, his glance lingering on her hair, her cheeks and her mouth.

'You look very lovely this morning,' he whispered, 'and I can't think why you would want to go to Green Cove.'

'Laurie says her father is willing to take me and Tony over to Seaton in his fishing boat. I . . . I . . . have to take Tony to the hospital there to have his head looked at,' she replied, speaking also in a whisper, unable to look away from him now, her own eyes expressing, although she did not know it, her appreciation of his appearance as their glances lingered on the thick springiness of his hair, the laughter lines at the corners of his eyes, the warm generous curves of his lips, the hard toughness of prominent cheekbones, aquiline nose and jutting chin, the proud set of muscular shoulder under the rough checked shirt and the strong column of his sunbronzed throat shadowed by the casually turned up open collar of his shirt.

'Hey, you two!' Tony pulled at her skirt to get her attention. 'I'm hungry and I want my lunch!'

Val's mouth quirked at one corner in a slight smile as he glanced sideways and down at their son.

'Then you run on to the house, Tony,' he ordered in quiet but firm tones. 'Your mummy and I will follow soon.'

To Karen's surprise Tony obeyed immediately and began to skip towards the house, his little fish flapping from its line. She remembered suddenly that Paul was still in the house and imagined Tony's reaction when he saw him.

'Tony, no, don't go in the house. Wait for Mummy,' she called out, turning away from the shed and beginning to run after him. She ran instead full tilt into Val, colliding violently with his hard, tensile body so that all the breath was knocked out of her. Her overnight bag slid from her shoulder. He dropped his fishing rod and sack and his arms went round her to hold her closely.

'I said we'd follow him,' he murmured, sliding one hand up her back and under her hair. His fingers trailed gently and seductively over her nape, under her ear and along her jawbone, each one of them titillating the tender nerve endings beneath the delicate skin so that she gasped again for breath in an agony of pleasure. 'We'll follow him after this,' he added softly, crooking one finger under her chin to lift it, and his parted lips claimed hers.

The heat of his mouth opening over hers melted the little resistance to him which was left in her. As he tilted her head sideways against the curve of his arm the blue sky, the fluffy white clouds, the twinkling leaves of a nearby tree swung above her and she closed her eyes so as to enjoy more fully the long ripples of sensuousness which were flowing through her body under the slow caress of his hands. Her hand reached up blindly yet unerringly to his throat and slid round to his nape so that her fingers could play in the thick, silky hair. Moulded closely together, they swayed slightly, shaken by the intensity of the passion which had leapt up between them, and for a few moments the rest of the world was of no account to either of them as they were lost together in a world of their own making.

Slowly and reluctantly Val withdrew his lips from hers only to hold her more closely, crushing her breasts with his hard chest, scraping the softness of her cheek with his bristly chin.

'I wanted to kiss you like that when we were in bed together last night,' he whispered huskily. 'I wanted to do it this morning when I woke up and found you still there beside me.'

'Why didn't you?' she asked. Her eyes still closed, she was still a little giddy, still overwhelmed by the eroticism induced by his close embrace.

'I sensed you weren't feeling very friendly towards me last night and before I was able to coax you into being friendly I fell asleep,' he replied, with a touch of self-mockery.

'And this morning?' she teased him.

'This morning I didn't have a chance to do what I wanted,' he said with a gruff laugh into the thickness of her hair. 'As soon as Tony woke up he came burrowing into our bed, determined to lie between us.'

'It isn't *our* bed,' Karen reminded him. She was reluctant to step away from him and was, in fact, clinging unashamedly to him, pressing her body against his in intimate invitation.

'It could be. You've only to say you'll marry me,' Val whispered, sliding his cheek from hers, turning his lips to hers, smothering with another scorching kiss any retort she might have made.

'Mummy, Mummy!' Tony's voice, raised to a screaming note, slashed through the delicious sensuous spell in which they had been caught, bringing them both back to reality. They pushed away from each other and turned towards him. He was running as fast as his little legs could carry him and even as they both started to go towards him he tripped over an unseen rock and went sprawling. Immediately he sat up and clutching his leg began to cry noisily.

'What's the matter? What happened?' cried Karen urgently as she bent down beside him.

'I hurt my knee!' he wailed, the tears streaming down his face.

'Let me look at it,' she said soothingly, sitting down on the grass beside him and pushing the right leg of the new stiff jeans he was wearing and which must have been bought for him by Val at the same time the pyjamas had been purchased. 'It looks a bit red, but there isn't a bump or a scratch,' she said, smiling at him as she pulled down the pants leg again and ruffled his hair. 'I think you'll live. But why were you screaming?'

'I saw Paul in the house. He said he's come to get you and take you back home. I don't want you to go with him.' Tony went on to his knees and put his arms around her. 'Please don't go with him, Mummy! Please stay here with Daddy and me. I want to live with my daddy, not with Paul.' A fresh burst of sobs shook his slight body and her arms went round him automatically to comfort him.

'When did Dutton arrive?' Val was standing beside them. He dropped her overnight bag to the ground near her and she looked up at him. He was staring at her with eyes that glittered with an icy green light and his mouth was curved into a tight bitter shape.

'About an hour ago,' she replied.

'Why didn't you tell me?'

'I . . . I don't know.' Karen shook her head and looked away from his piercing gaze.

'And is Tony right? Have you agreed to go back to Canada with Dutton and leave Tony here?'

'We . . . Paul and I did discuss what might be done,' she whispered honestly. There was no point in lying to him because Paul was coming out of the house, closing the porch door behind him and looking about. He saw them and began to walk across the grass towards them. 'But we agreed you would have to agree to such a suggestion too before any decision was taken.'

'No problem there,' Val replied coldly. 'It'll suit me fine if you leave Tony with me.'

'Karen, just what the hell is going on?' Paul sounded irritable. 'The boy came running into the house, took one look at me, threw a fish that hit me right in the face, and ran out screaming!'

Her feelings seesawing between hysterical amusement and anger, Karen looked at Tony, who had pushed away from her and was staring apprehensively at Paul.

'Tony, did you really throw a fish at Paul?'

The boy nodded his head fiercely and turning towards her hid his face against her shoulder again.

'That wasn't a very nice thing to do,' she chided him. 'And I think you should say you're sorry.' Behind her she could hear the throb of the pick-up's engine as it returned. Then it stopped as the ignition was turned off. Laurie had come back. 'Come on, Tony, say you're sorry to Paul,' she urged him.

'No!' The answer came out clearly enough, although Tony buried his face against her immediately and squirmed in her arms. Struggling to her knees, Karen managed to stand up. Tony clung to her leg, still hiding his face.

'Val, this is Paul Dutton,' she said stiffly and politely making the introduction. 'Paul, I'd like you to meet Valentine Knight.'

Paul nodded at Val and what she could only describe as a small cold smile curved his prim mouth. He didn't offer his right hand and neither did Val.

'I'm Karen's fiancé,' Paul announced. 'And you are, I believe, Tony's father.'

'That's right,' drawled Val. 'What are you doing here?'

'I followed Karen here because I thought I might

be able to help her come to terms with you about the custody of the child,' said Paul in his best lawyer's voice, sounding pompous and yet sincere. 'She tells me you're quite willing to take the responsibility of the child. Is that so?'

'Sure it is,' said Val, not bothering to hide his amusement at Paul's manner, his wide white grin creasing his lean cheeks attractively. 'That's why I brought Tony here.'

At that moment Laurie came round the corner of the house. She pulled up short when she saw them, then began to walk slowly towards them. She stopped a few yards away and stood with her hands in her jeans pockets watching and listening.

'Speaking as Karen's lawyer rather than as her fiancé,' Paul went on, 'I think it would be advantageous to all of us if you adopted Tony so that he could be recognised legally as your son and then there would be no problem about arranging for you to have legal custody of him once Karen is married to me. Would that be agreeable to you?'

Val's greenish-grey glance slanted from Paul's face to Karen's and then back again to Paul's.

'I'm not sure I understand what you mean when you say advantageous to us all,' he said softly. 'In what way would such an arrangement be advantageous to Karen?'

'Perhaps we could go into the house and I'll explain,' replied Paul smoothly, having become aware of Laurie's presence. 'I'm sure your housekeeper could keep an eye on Tony for half an hour while you and Karen and I discuss the matter.'

'Okay,' said Val. 'Let's go in.' And he began to

walk towards the house. Paul followed him, leaving
Karen with Tony and Laurie.

'I came back as soon as I realised they'd walked
back through the woods,' Laurie whispered,
coming over to Karen. 'What do you want to do
now? We could leave now, if you like, while they
aren't looking.'

'Go where?' Tony pushed away from Karen and
scowled up at her. 'Where will we go, Mummy?'

'To Seaton,' she whispered, watching Val open
the porch door and step into the house. 'To have
your head looked at at the hospital.' Now Paul
was entering the house. Picking up her overnight
bag, she slung it over her shoulder and taking
Tony's hand in hers began to run towards the gap
between the house and the generator shed. 'Come
on, Laurie!' she called.

'No, no!' screamed Tony, trying to tug his hand
free of hers. 'I don't want to go to hospital. I want
my lunch. I want to eat my fishy!'

'Be quiet!' Karen ordered sharply. 'You're
coming with me now.' Bending swiftly, she
managed to lift him and although she found him
heavy she managed to run after Laurie to the pick-
up truck.

'No, no!' yelled Tony, kicking his legs. 'I want
Daddy to come too. I want Daddy to come with
us!'

One hand across his mouth, feeling as if she was
now doing the kidnapping, Karen reached the
truck, heaved him up on to the seat through the
door Laurie had swung open, climbed up after him
and slammed the door shut. The engine was

already running and the truck was moving, reversing swiftly and then surging forward on to the road. Just before it turned she had a glimpse of Paul, running after it waving his arms.

'I want to go back, I want to go back!' wailed Tony, pummelling at Karen with his little fists. 'I want Daddy, I want my daddy!' He burst into tears again.

'Well, we did it,' said Laurie with a triumphant grin.

'Yes, we did it,' muttered Karen. But she was wondering as she tried to soothe her sobbing child whether her getaway with Tony was going to be worth the effort she had made to escape. Tony's cry for his father, his longing to stay with Val after knowing him for only a short time in preference to going away with her, hurt her bitterly, and yet she found in both an echo of her own cries and needs. She saw suddenly quite clearly that she also wanted Val to be with her, she wanted to stay with him. Then why had she run away?

The truck lurched along the dirt road between the close-growing trees. After a while the trees thinned out and the glitter of water appeared through their branches. The road curved out of the woods to swoop down towards a wide, almost landlocked bay. Wooden houses, most of them built in maritime style with steeply pitched roofs and high gable ends, were scattered about the head of the harbour, set on cleared land, bright with tawny grass and dying blueberry leaves.

Fishing boats, mostly painted white, bobbed on the glinting water, their bows all pointing in the direction of the land that sheltered them from the wind. Grey, weathered timbered fish-houses crouched above the water, supported by sturdy wooden pilings. Laurie drove off the road and down to the old wooden wharf, bringing the truck to a stop outside one of the fish-houses where some fishermen were lounging and talking.

One of the men, tall and grey-haired, detached himself from the group and came towards the pick-up truck. Swinging open the door on Karen's side, he helped her out of the truck, then lifted Tony down.

'This is Miss Carne, Dad,' said Laurie, coming round to them. 'And this is Tony.'

'Pleased to meet you,' drawled Murray Arnold, studying Karen with bright blue eyes. 'Laurie says you want to go to Seaton this afternoon.'

Karen hesitated, caught sight of Laurie staring at her and hesitated no longer.

'Yes, please,' she said.

'Cost you twenty bucks,' said Murray, in much the same way as Jerry had said it the day before.

'You can have it now,' she retorted, zipping open the outside pocket of her bag and taking out her wallet. 'I'd like to go at once.'

'Okay.' Murray's long-fingered hand curled round the twenty-dollar note. 'The boat's tied up at the float. I'll carry the boy down for you.'

'Goodbye, Miss Carne,' called Laurie as Karen followed Murray down the gangway that led to the slippery fish-scaled float.

'Goodbye, Laurie. Thanks for your help,' Karen replied, and stepped aboard the boat.

In the shelter of the wheelhouse she sat on a fish-box. Tony stood beside her, bent over, hiding his face in her lap. As the boat chugged down the bay she looked at the land across the sparkling water. Gradually the fish-sheds were losing their angular shape and becoming smudges of grey against the tawny-green grass of the slopes behind them and high up the houses were losing their identity too, becoming blobs of white, red, yellow and blue paint against the dark green of the forest.

The boat changed course and slowed down to pass through a narrow channel. Red-painted buoys appeared on one side and black rounded can buoys appeared on the other to show the edges of the channel. Beyond them reddish rocks festooned with olive-green rock-weed pierced the swirling and often splashing water. High on a dark headland stood the white tower of an old lighthouse with its gabled keeper's house, abandoned now, its windows boarded up.

Once the boat was through the channel Murray opened the engine's throttle. The boat's bow hit the wind-tossed sea with a crash and spray flew everywhere. Tony cried out and huddled closer to Karen as the boat went on pitching up and down and often rolled sickeningly sideways.

Feeling more alone than she had ever done in her life, Karen stared out over the heaving restless sea at the fast fading island. She had done what she had come to do. She had come for Tony and was taking him away with her, taking him away from his father. She had got her child back, but at a terrible cost, because she felt deep down that after what had happened today her relationship with Tony would never be the same. It would be a long, long time before he trusted her again, because she had taken him away from someone he had always secretly wished to know and be with. She had taken him away from Val.

CHAPTER SIX

AN hour later, in the neat brick building of the small hospital that overlooked the harbour at Seaton, Karen helped Tony to dress himself again after he had been examined by the young doctor who was on duty for the weekend. All through the examination Tony had been silently yet sullenly well-behaved. Now he looked at her, his grey eyes curiously blank and cold.

'Can we go back to the island, now, to stay with Daddy?' he asked. 'The doctor says I'm all right.'

'I think we should both have something to eat first, don't you?' she replied, putting off for as long as she could telling him that they would not be returning to Big Spruce Island but would be driving back to Canada as soon as possible. 'We haven't had any lunch and I'm very hungry, aren't you?'

He nodded as she zipped up his jacket and turned his head to see who was coming back into the room as the door swung open. The doctor, slim and trim in his white coat, grinned down at him.

'Sorry we can't do more for him, Mrs Carne,' he said. 'But he seems okay to me, lucid and talking sensibly. We don't have a brain scanner here, so I suggest that as soon as you get back to where you live you go to your own doctor and see if he can fix up a brain scan for Tony in one of your hos-

pitals. Only that way can you be really sure there's
been no serious damage to the brain—internal
bleeding, that sort of thing, you know. Are you
going straight back to Canada?'

'Er—yes,' said Karen. 'At least, as soon as we've
had a meal.'

'Try Sadie's in the Main Street. It's the only
place open in the village this time of the year, but
you'll get good home-made chowder there and
good sandwiches,' replied the doctor cheerfully,
holding open the door so that she and Tony could
go through. 'Stop at the information desk as you
go out of here and they'll give you a bill for the
consultation. Have a good day, now.'

Karen paid for the consultation with some of
the cash she had brought with her and after putting
her receipt away took hold of Tony's hand and
walked out of the hospital, pausing on the steps
for a few moments wondering whether to go in her
car to Sadie's or whether to leave it parked where
it was. In the end she decided to walk up to the
Main Street and set off up the hill.

'Karen, Karen!'

She swung round in surprise. Behind her Paul
was huffing and puffing up the slope from the harbour. Behind him the water in the bay shimmered
with bright reflected sunlight.

'How . . . how did you get here?' she exclaimed.
Beside her Tony cringed away from Paul as he
came to a stop in front of her.

'Knight brought me over in his motorboat as
soon as we both realised you'd come here,' he
replied breathlessly, taking out a handkerchief and

wiping his brow. 'Why did you go off like that?' he demanded.

Karen looked past him down the slope which was shaded by tall elm trees to the bright harbour. There was no sign of Val.

'Has Val gone back to the island?' she asked.

'No. He said something about going to visit a relative of his who owns a hotel. Karen, you haven't answered me. Why did you go off like that?'

'I'd made an arrangement to come over here with Laurie's father so I could go to the hospital with Tony to have his head examined,' she replied coolly, turning to face the hill again and beginning to walk up it. 'The doctor there gave him a thorough check-up and said he's all right but that I should arrange for a brain scan as soon as I get back home.'

'You are going back to Canada, then?' asked Paul, matching his steps to hers and Tony's, still breathing heavily after his run to catch up with her.

'Yes,' she replied stiffly. Where else could she go?

'And you've decided to take Tony with you?'

'I have. We're just going to have our lunch. Tony hasn't had any at all. There's a restaurant in the Main Street. Are you coming with us?'

Paul looked at his watch.

'Quarter after three,' he murmured. 'I guess I have time for a cup of coffee with you. The last flight for Montreal leaves soon after six and I have a reservation on it. I'm also booked on a flight from Montreal to Toronto this evening. I've an important meeting in the city tomorrow morning. Will you be all right, driving back on your own?'

'I was all right coming, wasn't I?' she retorted coolly. 'But I won't set off this evening. Tony and I will stay at a motel here and start off bright and early tomorrow.'

'Then you should be home by tomorrow evening. I'll call you as soon as I get home from the office to find out if you're back.'

They reached the top of the hill and looked along the Main Street. The plate glass of shop windows glinted back at them. Above the shop fronts the pointed gables of the buildings were painted blue, yellow or white. All had neat black shutters edging their upstairs windows. Outside one of the blue buildings a swinging sign glinted. On the sign was painted a picture of two seagulls and above the picture were printed the words 'Sadie's Pantry.'

Inside the small dining area they sat at a table covered with a blue and white checked cloth close to a window. Karen unzipped Tony's parka and unbuttoned her suit jacket. A waitress brought them menus. Karen ordered fish chowder for herself and Tony, to be followed by a club sandwich between them, and Paul ordered coffee.

'Mummy,' whispered Tony, 'I want to go to the rest-room.'

'All right.' She stood up. 'I'll take you to it.'

She left him in the men's toilet and returned to the table across the polished floor, made from strips of oak. The restaurant was very clean and had a pleasant atmosphere with its panelled walls and trailing green plants growing in hanging pots.

Paintings of sailing boats, lobster traps and buoys, lighthouses and rocks done by a local artist decorated the walls, and she was studying one of them which hung on a wall nearby the table where she was sitting, wondering if it was a painting of the lighthouse at Big Spruce Island, when Paul spoke to her.

'Karen, I wish I knew what's going on in your mind,' he said with an exasperated sigh. 'On the island you said you'd like to discuss with Knight the possibility of leaving Tony with him. Now you've just told me you're returning to Canada and taking Tony with you. I think you owe me an explanation of your extremely erratic behaviour.'

'You're right—I do owe you an explanation,' she said, giving him a rueful smile. She rested her hands on the table, taking hold of the fingers of the left with the fingers of the right. She had good hands, square-palmed and long-fingered, white-skinned with shining almond-shaped nails. On the third finger of her left hand the diamond ring Paul had given her when she had agreed to marry him glittered opulently as she twisted it and then began to pull it off. Holding it between her finger and thumb, she turned it so that the diamond twinkled with reflected coloured light.

'It's very pretty,' she commented, 'the only ring a man has ever given me, but I've decided I don't want it after all, so I'm returning it to you.' Leaning over, she placed the ring on the table in front of him. 'That's my explanation,' she added. 'I've come to the conclusion that I don't want to marry you after all. I'm sorry, Paul, but I don't think it would work.'

He stared down at the ring, then looked up at her, his brow creased with crooked worry lines, his brown eyes looking very mournful, like those of a dog which has been refused a walk or a bone. The waitress came back to set the places with knives and forks and glasses of water, and he snatched the ring up and put it in his pocket.

'Why?' he whispered, his head poking forward from his shoulders as he stared at Karen. 'You've got to tell me why.'

She waited until the waitress had gone away before replying and then she spoke carefully, weighing every word, not wanting to hurt him too much.

'I've decided that it would be selfish of me to inflict Tony on you,' she replied. 'You're accustomed to living on your own and even when you were married before you didn't take kindly to being a father. Some men don't . . . just as some women don't take to being mothers.'

'But . . . but . . . we can solve that problem by leaving the boy with his real father, who happens to want him,' Paul spluttered. 'We were very close to solving it when you walked out on Knight and me before we could come to any terms. You know, Karen, I'm beginning to think that you walked out and came over to Seaton because you didn't want to discuss the matter.'

'You're quite right, I did,' she whispered. 'You see, I realised I can't give Tony up for you. I can't leave him with Val so that I can marry you and I can't send him away to a boarding school so that you and I can be alone, so there's only one way

out. I won't marry you at all. I see now that
I shouldn't have agreed to marry you at all,
and I apologise for having accepted your proposal.'

'Karen, you're upset,' said Paul, leaning towards
her urgently. 'Knight has upset you, kidnapping
the boy the way he did, bringing him here.'

'I know I'm upset, but maybe I needed to be
upset so that I would see more clearly what I was
about to do,' she replied. 'I was going to make a
mistake which would have hurt all of us—you, me,
Tony and Val.'

'And do you really believe you're not hurting
anyone by what you're doing now?' he exclaimed.
'What about Tony? He's already formed quite an
attachment to his father. Don't you think he's been
hurt today?'

'I know he's been hurt,' she said miserably, 'but
there isn't anything I can do about it. I couldn't
leave him with Val. I couldn't say goodbye to him
and drive back to Canada. I couldn't!' Her voice
choked and she searched in her suit pocket for a
handkerchief to blow her nose. 'Please, Paul, try to
understand,' she pleaded.

'Oh, I do understand, much better than you
think,' he retorted with a touch of dryness. 'You're
in love with Knight, that's really why you don't
want to marry me any more.'

'I'm not,' she argued feebly.

'I doubt very much if you've ever stopped being
in love with him,' he went on. 'Oh, you've done a
good job of pretending, covered up with that dis-
guise you're so good at hiding behind, the mask of

the cool, collected career woman.' His mouth took on an unpleasant curve. 'Perhaps after all I should be grateful to Knight for snatching his child from you this weekend. It's certainly shown you up in a new light to me and made me realise exactly where I stand in your affections. I'm right at the bottom of the list, and quite frankly, Karen, that's not a place I like to be.' He pushed his chair back and stood up. 'I don't think I want coffee after all. Thanks for returning the ring—I appreciate that. I'll be on my way to the airport now.' Briefcase in hand, he stood for a moment, slanting a glance in her direction. 'On second thoughts I won't give you a call tomorrow evening to see if you've returned. This is goodbye, Karen.'

'Goodbye, Paul,' she whispered, making no effort to detain him, feeling relief flood through her because he was going out of her life; because she wouldn't have to fight him over the matter of sending Tony to a boarding school; because she wouldn't have to marry him.

'Here we are at last!' The waitress was back with a loaded tray. She glanced at the door which was closing behind Paul. 'Won't the gentleman be staying for his coffee?'

'No. He has to catch a plane in Bangor. I'll have his coffee,' said Karen.

'And what about the little boy? Has he gone too?'

'Tony? Oh, no, he's just in the rest-room. Perhaps I'd better go and see if he's all right,' said Karen, realising that Tony had been in the men's room for the best part of fifteen minutes.

She left the table and went down the passageway where the rest-rooms were located. Pausing outside the men's, she rapped with her knuckles on the door.

'Tony!' she called. 'Are you all right? Are you coming out now? Your chowder's on the table and it smells good!'

There was no reply and the door remained closed. Karen knocked and called his name again. Still nothing happened. Cautiously she pushed the door open and looked around the edge of it. There was no one in the rest-room. Closing the door, Karen hurried back, expecting to see Tony sitting at their table in the seat nearest to the window, but every chair was empty and the food on the table was untouched. She looked round at the other tables. A young couple, obviously lovers from the way they were looking at one another, were the only other people in the room and Tony wasn't with them. She went over to them.

'Excuse me, but were you here before I came in?' she asked.

They turned their heads and looked at her rather pityingly as if they thought she was a little crazy.

'No. You were here before us,' replied the young woman. 'You were sitting over there with an older man.'

'I was wondering if you noticed my little boy. He ... he went to the rest-room, but he isn't there now and he hasn't come back.'

'He wasn't with you when we came in,' said the young woman. 'And I haven't seen anyone come from the rest-room. Was there anyone in the men's when you were in there, Fred?'

'No.' The young man shook his head from side to side 'But I saw a little guy running down the hill towards the harbour when we came up the steps into this place.'

'Did he have a lot of black hair?' asked Karen.

'I dunno.' The young man, whose hair was long and brown and curly, shrugged his shoulders and looked at the young woman with a mocking expression on his face. 'I wasn't close enough to him to see.'

He and the young woman became absorbed in each other again, deliberately ignoring Karen, and she turned back to the table.

'Everything okay, ma'am?' asked the waitress, bustling up.

'No, it isn't. I can't find my little boy. He isn't in the rest-room and he didn't return to the table. Have you seen him?'

'No.'

'I'll have to go outside and look for him.'

'But what about the food?' exclaimed the waitress, following Karen as she hurried towards the door. 'You can't go without paying for it, you know.'

'But....' began Karen, swinging round. The fierce expression on the waitress's face made her bite back what she was going to say. 'Oh, all right,' she sighed. 'Do you have the bill made out?'

She paid for the food she and Tony hadn't eaten and was assured by the waitress that it would be kept until they returned to the restaurant. She stepped out of the door and ran down the steps, crossed the road and began to hurry down the hill towards the harbour, convinced that the 'little guy' the young man in the restaurant had seen had been Tony, on his way to the harbour in the hopes of finding Val there, preparing to go back to Big Spruce Island in his motorboat. The little devil must have slipped out of the restaurant when she and Paul had been talking, when they had both been so engrossed in their argument they hadn't noticed him.

There were a few people on the fishermen's wharf, some of them fishing with rod and line, some of them walking about enjoying the fresh air and sunshine and some of them just lounging. Karen walked the full length of the wharf, peering down into the few boats that were tied up, re- cognising Val's boat immediately because it was black and had a distinctive red stripe painted on each side, just under the rail. Tony wasn't in the boat, nor was he anywhere on the wharf as far as she could tell. As she walked back she stopped occasionally to ask some of the fishermen and some of the loungers if they had seen him. Only one of them thought he had, and he couldn't be sure in which direction Tony had been going.

Worried sick by this time, Karen walked to her car, which was still parked outside the hospital. Tony wasn't in the parking lot and he couldn't have got into the car, because it was locked. Unlocking the door, she slid in behind the steering wheel. There was only one course left open to her before she asked for police assistance. She would drive around the town, hoping to spot Tony walking along.

After having driven along the few avenues without seeing him she decided to drive out along the road which wound around the bay in the direction of Allan's Point. There was just a chance that Tony had found Val and was now at the inn with his father.

Was it only yesterday that she had driven this way? So much had happened in such a short time—more, so it seemed to her, than had happened during the past seven years, and all because Val had come storming back into her life and had snatched her child away from her. No, he had snatched *their* child away from her, and it was beginning to look as if he had snatched Tony from her again. But how? How could he have taken Tony from the restaurant without either her or Paul seeing him enter and leave?

The road dipped down to the cleared land of the point which looked exactly as it had looked yesterday, only the shadows of the trees were longer and the sun shone full upon the front of the house. Washing was still flapping on the line at the back of the house and someone was still hammering shingles on. Karen got out of the car, felt her head whirl and staggered slightly. For a moment she leaned against the car until she felt steadier, realising that hunger was causing the feeling of weakness.

When her head had stopped whirling she walked over to the hotel and pressed the button of the door-bell beside the front door. After a while the door opened. Sue Allan stood in the opening. She held a baby of about three months in her arms, and her clear grey glance was as cool and hostile as ever.

'I'm sorry to bother you,' said Karen, 'but I was told that Val had come here. I . . . I'd like to speak to him, please.'

'He's gone for a walk,' replied Sue coolly, hitching the baby up against her shoulder and patting his back. Her blouse was unbuttoned at the front and she had obviously been feeding the child.

'Oh. Do you know if he . . . he has a little boy with him?' asked Karen. The strange headache had returned and dark spots had begun to dance before her eyes.

'No. He's by himself,' said Sue shortly.

'Then perhaps you'd tell me which way he's gone,' pleaded Karen. She saw Sue's face close up even more and blurted out, 'Please, please tell me! I . . . I . . . can't find my little boy. I've lost him and I thought . . . I was hoping Val might know where he is or would help me find him. You see, he's . . . Tony is Valentine's son too.'

'I know he is,' replied Sue, her face softening slightly as she shifted the baby again so that he was cradled in her arms. Burping happily, he blinked up at her.

'How old is he?' Karen asked huskily, remembering Tony when he was a baby, studying the way the dark hair grew on the child's head, admiring the soft pink of his skin and the fragile starlike shapes of his tiny hands as he waved them about.

'Two and a half months. We've called him Benjamin because he's so well-beloved,' said Sue softly, then looked up and straight at Karen, her glance hostile again. 'I wonder if you know much you've hurt Val by keeping his son from him, by not telling him about Tony's birth and allowing him to share in his own child's growth and development.'

'I know now,' whispered Karen. 'He's made it very clear to me by the way he's behaved this weekend.'

'Then why did you take Tony away from him today?' demanded Sue. 'Why are you going back to Canada with another man and taking Tony with you?'

'I . . . I'm not going back to Canada with another man,' muttered Karen. Her head had started to whirl again and she was having great difficulty in speaking. She was becoming overwhelmed by a great desire to lie down there and then on the ground in front of Sue. In fact she was sliding down and her eyes were closing. Far away she heard a voice that sounded like Val's call her name, so she opened her eyes and looked round. The last thing she saw were the brown leather of the boots he was wearing and the coarse weave of his denim jeans.

She came round as he was laying her down on a softly cushioned chesterfield which was drawn close to a black Franklin stove. The doors of the stove were open and a bright log fire blazed in it behind the mesh of a fireguard.

'What happened?' Karen asked in puzzlement.

Val's arms released her, but he remained kneeling beside the couch, looking down at her, his black eyebrows slanting in a frown, the expression in his eyes one of concern.

'You passed out, just folded up at Sue's feet. I saw it happen as I came round the corner of the house. Do you know why it happened?'

Karen's hand went to her brow to lift back her hair. The black cloud was still hovering, threatening to overcome her again, and it was going to take all her strength to answer him.

'I . . . I . . . haven't had much to eat today, only half a sandwich and a cup of coffee,' she whispered. 'We were in the restaurant and the waitress had just brought the chowder. I went to get Tony from the rest-room, but he wasn't there. Oh, Val, I've lost him! I've lost him!' she cried wildly, lunging up on her elbows. 'I looked everywhere for him and I couldn't find him. Please, will you go and look for him again, help me to find him?'

She was shaking all over and tears were running down her face. Val reached out and pulled her against him.

'Hush, honey,' he murmured. 'Calm down and tell me exactly what happened. I have to know so that I can understand Tony's behaviour and guess from that what was in his mind when he ran away from you. Because you must realise that's what he's done. He's run away from you because he didn't like what you were going to do. We'll start with what happened at the hospital.'

'Don't you think she should have something to eat first before you start questioning her?' The voice was Sue's, and raising her head from the comforting support of Val's shoulder Karen looked up. Sue was standing at the end of the chesterfield with a small tray between her hands. On the tray was a bowl containing something that steamed. 'I've brought some soup for you,' she said, coming forward. 'It's beef and vegetable and I made it myself. Afterwards you can have a poached egg on toast, if you like, and a glass of milk.'

'Thank you,' Karen whispered, wiping away the tears from her cheeks with the backs of her hands. Val moved away from her and she sat up, swinging her legs down so that her feet rested on the floor. Val brought a small occasional table and set it close to her, and Sue placed the tray on the table and left the room.

The soup was hot, and the roll of bread beside it fresh and crusty. Karen ate several spoonfuls of the soup and all of the roll, aware that Val was sitting beside her watching her. At last he said,

'What did the doctor at the hospital say about Tony?'

'He said he was all right but that I should arrange for a brain scan as soon as I could see Tony's doctor at home,' she said.

'And then you left the hospital.'

'Yes. I . . . we . . . Tony and I were going to the restaurant to eat because he was very hungry too.' She turned to him anxiously. 'Oh, Val, he could have passed out too with hunger. He could be lying somewhere in a faint. Oh, we must go and find him, we must!'

'You're not going anywhere. You're going to stay here. I'll go and find him,' he said in a hard authoritative voice. 'What did you say to him when you left the hospital? Did you tell him you were going to take him back to Canada?'

'No. He . . . he asked me if we were going back to the island and I said we should both have something to eat first, and then Paul turned up. He asked me if we were going back to Canada and I told him. . . .' Her glance faltered away from Val's intent piercing gaze. 'I told him yes, we were.'

'So Tony would hear you say that.'

'Yes, I suppose he would only I didn't think he was listening. Then we all went to the restaurant. After we'd ordered the meal Tony asked to go to the rest-room. I showed him where it was and left him there and went back to the table.'

'And?' Against her jaw Val's fingers were hard and strong, forcing her face up, making her look at him. 'You've got to tell me everything, Karen. No more secrets.'

'Paul said . . . well, he and I had a disagreement,' she whispered. 'He . . . he. . . . wasn't pleased with the way I'd behaved since . . . since I'd found out you'd kidnapped Tony. On the island he'd told me that he didn't want Tony to live with us after we got married. He said he hoped I would either leave Tony with you or send him to a boarding school.' Karen's fingers gripped one another on her lap. 'I . . . I gave him his ring back and told him I didn't want to marry him any more,' she muttered.

Val's eyebrows flickered up in surprise. Taking hold of her left hand, he examined it. Keeping the hand in his warm grasp, he glanced at her again, his eyes no longer cold and wary.

'And all the time you were talking to Dutton,

Tony was in the rest-room,' he drawled.

'I thought he was.'

'But he wasn't. He either walked out right past you while you were too engrossed in your argument with Dutton to notice him or he found another way to leave the restaurant,' he said thoughtfully. Although his gaze remained steadily directed towards her face his fingers were fondling her hand, straying over the palm to the wrist, stroking the delicate skin there, sending tingles of pleasure dancing along her arm. She tried to pull her hand free, and at once his fingers lost their gentle seductive touch and turned into steel, forming a manacle around her wrist. 'No, sweetheart,' he whispered, leaning towards her to touch his lips to hers in a swift yet seductive kiss. 'You're caught now, caught and bound, and I'm never going to let you get away again.' He drew back from her. 'Where's Dutton now?'

'He left for Bangor to catch a plane soon after I gave him back his ring. That's when I went to look for Tony.'

'Did you ask anyone if they'd seen Tony?'

'Yes, I asked as many people as I could. Only a young man who was in the restaurant thought he might have seen him. He said he'd seen a little boy running down to the harbour, and that's where I went first. I thought he'd gone to look for you. I drove along all the streets but didn't see him anywhere. Then I remembered Paul had said you'd told him you were going to visit a relative and I decided to come here. I thought that perhaps Tony had found you and you'd brought him here.' Her lips trembled slightly and tears sprang into her eyes. 'But he isn't here, is he?'

'No, he isn't here, but he will be soon, because I'm going right now to find him.' Releasing her hand, Val rose to his feet. 'I'll have to use your car. Where are the keys?'

'In the ignition. I'll come with you.' Karen began to get to her feet, but everything whirled around her again and she flopped back. Her hands covering her face, she began to weep. 'I can't come with you. I can't come,' she moaned.

'You don't have to come.' Val sat down beside her again and took her in his arms again. 'I'll find him.' He rubbed his cheek against hers. 'You've got to stop giving him reasons to run away, Karen. Think about that while I'm gone.'

He kissed her again, another warm but swift caress, the sort of kiss he might have given Sue, Karen thought, or any other woman who was in need of comfort. With a few long strides he had left the room, she heard him talking to someone outside the door of the room and then a few seconds later the front door of the house slammed as he shut it.

'How are you feeling now?' Sue appeared with another small tray.

'Still weak and wobbly,' said Karen, trying to smile and failing miserably because her lips trembled again and tears began to drip down her cheeks. 'I can't understand it. Nothing like this has ever happened to me before. I've never fainted in my life before this.'

'I guess you've been under a lot of stress during

the past two days,' replied Sue, doing a deft juggling act as she removed the tray with the soup bowl from the table and put down the other tray. 'Eat up,' she ordered lightly. 'And then put your feet up and rest. You can depend on Val to do his best to find Tony.'

'You're very kind,' said Karen, picking up the knife and fork and beginning to attack the poached egg on toast. 'I know you don't like me, and. . . .'

'That isn't true,' said Sue in her soft yet sensible way. 'It's what you've done to Val in the past and just recently that I don't like.' She sat down cross-legged on the floor, looking like a teenage girl with her long braid hanging over one shoulder, her perfectly oval face and her serious grey gaze. 'You're really very different from what I'd always imagined you to be,' she added quietly.

'Oh!' Karen looked up quickly, slightly disconcerted. 'What did you imagine I was like?' she asked.

'Hard and selfish, a real Women's Libber,' said Sue with a little self-mocking grin. 'A sort of female chauvinist, believing yourself superior to men and taking all you could get from a man in sexual satisfaction without giving anything return. A real monster, in fact.' Her chuckle was attractively infectious, and Karen looked up again from the food she was eating to smile in understanding. 'But now I've met you I'm beginning to realise you're not like that at all. Underneath all that slick sophistication you're just like any other woman longing to love and be loved in return.'

Karen laid down her knife and fork, picked up

the glass of milk and drank. She was beginning to feel a little more like herself.

'I suppose Val told you about ... our ... our affair,' she murmured.

'No. You should know that Val never talks much about himself. Oh, I knew that he'd lived with a woman in London for a while, but I'd no idea how close his relationship had been with her until last June. You see, after you and your mother had left he told me who you were and that Tony was his son. He told me then that he was going to do everything he possibly could to get custody of Tony and have the boy live with him, even if it meant....' Sue broke off, her glance sliding away from Karen's face, and she frowned. 'Perhaps I shouldn't say it,' she muttered.

'You'll have to now,' remarked Karen dryly.

'I guess I will, won't I?' said Sue with a rueful grin. 'He said even if it meant having to marry you to get what he wanted. Has he asked you to marry him?'

'Yes, he has,' whispered Karen. 'And I realise he wants to marry me so he can claim Tony as his child and for no other reason.'

'What I can't understand is why you didn't get in touch with Val as soon as you knew you were pregnant with his child,' said Sue. 'I guess I must seem pretty naïve and a bit of a country bumpkin to you, but when I knew I was going to have my first baby I couldn't wait to tell Titus.'

'But ... but your situation was different from mine,' argued Karen. 'You were married to Titus. You and he had vowed to love and cherish each

other, to have a family. Val and I had made no
such vows to each other. The vows we'd made were
different. We had agreed not to tie any knots. We
were free to end our arrangement any time one of
us felt like it, and that's exactly what happened. It
wasn't until after we'd parted that I found out that
I was expecting a baby.' Karen looked at the flames
leaping up in the black stove. 'I would have liked
to rush to Val to tell him, to share the good news
with him,' she whispered. 'But I couldn't—I
couldn't. I was afraid.'

'Afraid of what?'

'I was afraid he might think that I'd got pregnant deliberately to trap him into marrying me,
and I knew he didn't want to be married just then,'
muttered Karen.

'Oh, you fool! You silly, proud fool!' said Sue.
'And he was as silly and proud as you were, not
keeping in touch with you, not going to Canada to
find you, which is what he wanted to do after his
first book had been published.'

'How do you know he wanted to do that?' exclaimed Karen.

'Because he told me, last June when I asked him
why he hadn't written to you or gone to see you.
He said the same as you, that you'd made no com-
mitments to each other, that you'd both been free
to change your minds, to stop loving when you
wanted, and he'd assumed when he didn't hear
from you again that you'd changed your mind
about him. He assumed you'd found someone else
to love, and that was okay by him if it was what
you wanted to do. It wouldn't take him long to

find himself someone else to love either.' Sue rose to her feet and began to transfer the soup bowl from one tray to the other and put the full tray on top of the empty one. Holding both trays in front of her, she looked down at Karen, a pitying expression in her eyes. 'There've been a couple of other women since you—Val isn't the type to remain celibate for long, you know, but neither of them could hold his interest. Now is there anything else I can get you?'

'No, thanks.'

'Then put your feet up and rest. I'm going to prepare a couple of bedrooms. You and Tony might as well stay the night here and I expect Val will too. I wonder how long it will take Val to find the boy?'

Sue went from the room and Karen did as she had been told and swung her legs up on to the chesterfield. She rested her head back against the cushion behind her and let a long sigh come out. For a while she stared at the fire, her mind seeming to revolve in circles from one errant thought to another. Faster and faster the circle turned, like a roulette wheel spinning round and round. She closed her eyes to try and stop it and was just slipping into a fitful doze when a hand shook her shoulder.

'Karen!' Sue's voice was urgent. 'Wake up! Val has found Tony.'

'Where?' Her eyes flew open and she sat up immediately. Sue looked very serious. 'Oh, he's all right, isn't he? He isn't . . . he isn't. . . .' She found her lips wouldn't shape the word dead.

'Yes, he's all right. The State police have him. One of them out on patrol saw him race across the street from the restaurant and down to the harbour and followed him. They've been waiting for you to call them and report him missing. They allowed Val one phone call and he says to ask you to go in to Seaton to explain. Titus says he'll drive you in now.'

'But what do they want me to explain?' asked Karen, rising to her feet, relieved to find that the black cloud had gone from above her eyes and that she was able to stand upright easily. 'Why can't they let Val bring Tony here?'

'Because they've put Val under arrest,' said Sue.

'They arrested him? Why?'

'It seems your friend Paul Dutton told them yesterday that Val had kidnapped Tony and had brought him here against your wishes, so they're holding Val on that charge until you go and deny it.'

CHAPTER SEVEN

In the bedroom she had shared with Tony in June when they had stayed at the Allan's Point Inn Karen sat on the edge of one of the twin beds and read the last line of a story from a book of children's stories which Sue had lent her. When she had finished reading she looked at Tony. He was fast asleep, his cheeks pink, his brow serene and white under the fronds of black hair, his eyelashes thick and black; a picture of innocence, he looked as if he were incapable of blackmail and would never think of running away from her just to make her do what he wanted.

'Why, Tony? Why did you run away this afternoon?' she had asked him when he had rushed towards her as soon as she had walked into the police station earlier that evening. She had bent to embrace him and had whispered the words into his ear.

''Cos you were going to take me back to Canada and 'cos you're going to marry Paul,' he had replied simply and clearly, looking up at her with limpid grey eyes.

'I'm not going to marry Paul,' she had replied, 'but we still have to go back to Canada. We live there and you have to go to school there.'

'No,' he had replied loudly, pushing away from her and going over to Val, who had been lounging casually against a big desk littered with papers. 'I'm not going back with you. I'm going to stay with Daddy. And you can marry him now that you're not going to marry Paul, and stay with us on the island.'

Aware suddenly that everything that she and Tony had been saying to each other had been listened to not only by Val but also by the two uniformed policemen who were in the room, Karen had felt hot colour rush into her cheeks. Across the space that had separated them her eyes had met Val's. Mockery had glinted briefly in his, then had faded away leaving them hard and cold, and she had realised then that for all his casual stance he had been furiously angry because he had been detained by the police.

It had taken nearly an hour for her to persuade the police that Val had not kidnapped Tony; that he had taken Tony away from the school and had brought him to Big Spruce Island with her permission. She had had to pretend that her relationship with him over the past few years had been much closer than it had been and that they had often met, and in the end she had had to admit that they were considering getting married. But she had been able to say truthfully and somewhat angrily that in going to the police and telling them that Val had kidnapped his own son Paul had been acting without her authority and knowledge.

It had been well after eight o'clock when at last she, Tony and Val had been able to leave Seaton and drive back to the inn. Val had done the driving and had been noticeably silent and withdrawn.

Tony, on the other hand, hadn't stopped talking, telling her how he had nearly been knocked down by the police car when he had run across the street leading down to the harbour; about how kind the policemen had been to him, sending out for hamburgers and french fries for him when he had complained of hunger and how they'd let him watch the T.V.

'I think you should stop telling your mother about the good time you've had and say you're sorry for running away from her,' Val had interrupted Tony suddenly and harshly. 'She's been very worried about you. Don't ever run away from her like that again, do you hear?'

'Ye-yes,' Tony had been shocked into saying.

'Then let me hear you say you're sorry,' Val had insisted.

'I . . . I'm sorry I ran away, Mummy,' Tony had muttered, curling his arms about her, burying his face in her breast.

'And?' Val had prompted coldly.

'And I . . . I won't ever do it again,' whispered Tony.

'I hope you won't, darling. I hope that . . . that neither your father nor I will ever give you cause to run away from either of us,' she had told him.

'Then you'll have to get married to each other, won't you?' said Tony, refusing to be defeated, and having the last word after all.

The rest of the drive had been completed in silence. When they had arrived at the inn Karen had taken Tony straight upstairs to see that he bathed and then saw him to bed dressed in a pair of pyjamas which Sue told him belonged to his cousin David Allan, her elder son, who was just seven years of age and who was staying that week end with his grandmother and grandfather but who would be back the next day.

'Will I be here to meet David?' Tony had asked as Karen had tucked him into bed, but his request had not been directed to her. Tony had been looking at Val, who had come into the bedroom to say goodnight to him.

'I don't know,' Val had replied coolly. 'It depends on your mother.'

He had wished Tony goodnight and had kissed him, then had left the room. Karen supposed he had gone downstairs. She put the book she had been reading from on the bedside table, turned down the lamp so that it didn't shine so brightly on Tony's face and stood up. It was almost eleven o'clock and she guessed everyone else had gone to bed. Going over to the other bed, she unzipped her overnight bag and took out her nightgown and the thin tissue-like kimono-styled dressing gown she always carried with her when she travelled because it packed easily. Quickly she stripped, pulled on the kimono and, toilet bag in hand, she went along the dimly lit landing to the bathroom.

When she emerged half an hour later, her skin still slightly damp and smelling of lavender from the soap and bath oil she had used, the landing was in complete darkness except for the shaft of light slanting out from Tony's room like a beacon beckoning to her and showing her the way. The house was quiet, but it wasn't the silence of a deserted place. Clocks ticked, people breathed. In fact Karen was sure she could hear someone breathing quite close to her as she tiptoed along the landing.

When a hand touched her arm she nearly screamed. Instead her breath came out in a loud gasp and she dropped her toilet bag. The hand, which was warm and strong, slid down her arm and scooped her hand into its grasp.

'Come in here for a while,' Val whispered, and led her into a bedroom illuminated by the moon which shed silver light on antique furniture, on an oval mirror, on dainty china ornaments, on water-colour paintings hanging on the walls and on the colourful old quilt made from narrow strips of velvet which covered the wide bed.

Val kicked the door closed behind him and Karen turned to look at him. Wearing only brief underpants, he was silvered too, the bright moon radiance giving his skin an unearthly supernatural shining quality, highlighting the muscular symmetry of his shoulders, chest and arms and accentuating the hollows and angles of his face. From beneath his heavy frowning black eyebrows and the thick fans of his eyelashes his eyes glinted with green fire; a demoniacal blaze that caused her to step back from him as she tried to pull her hand free of his.

'What do you want?' she whispered.

'You.' The curve to his lips was mocking and sensual. His hand tightened on hers and he drew her towards him. 'I'd like you to sleep with me again tonight.'

'But I have a bed in the other room. There are twin beds in there. I don't have to share one with Tony . . . or with you,' she replied coolly, trying to pull her hand free of his again to twist away from him, her hair flirting out in moon-glittering waves brushing across his face tormentingly as he bent his head towards her. 'I don't have to sleep with you. I'm not your wife,' she added, aware that her senses were beginning to quiver in response to his nearness, warning her that instinctively and physically she wanted him as much as he said he wanted her.

'You don't have to, I agree, but I think you would like it if we did,' Val murmured, and taking hold of her other hand he lifted both her hands, one at a time, to his lips, kissing them in silent homage while he still looked at her. 'We'll take it slowly and easily and it will be like nothing either of us has ever known before,' he said thickly, and then his lips were against hers, smothering any answer she might have made.

Dropping one of her hands, he groped for and found the knot which tied the sash of her kimono. A few deft pulls and it was undone. The edges of the silky kimono slid apart, exposing her lavender-scented, white-skinned body. His arms went around her and as her taut uplifted breasts felt the caress of his warm bare chest and his hips thrust against hers in subtle invitation something seemed to snap within her.

All the passionate feelings which she had kept locked up for seven years surged through her in a hot flood rising to her brain, intoxicating her and drowning all reasonable thought. Her hands linked behind his head, she pressed avidly against him, rubbing against him until he groaned gaspingly with pleasure. In a few moments Karen had changed from the cool, level-headed, almost sexless person she had prided herself in being for the past few years into a purely sensual woman, glorying in her knowledge of her mature and softly rounded body, luxuriating in the way it was coming alive under the tender touch of Val's fingers.

'It's good to be close to you again,' he murmured against her lips, then her nostrils were filled suddenly with the mind-drugging scents of his hair as he bent to nibble her throat with his lips. 'For a long time after you left me I used to dream about being with you. I missed you like hell, Karen,' he added, raising his head to look down into her eyes again, and now the green fire which moonlight had sparked from his eyes no longer seemed demoniacal to her. She recognized it as the hot blaze of passionate desire.

'Then why didn't you follow me to Canada? Why didn't you come to me?' she whispered, pressing against him again, her hands sliding tantalisingly over the silken smoothness of his bare back, fingers seeking for vulnerable hollows.

'God knows,' he groaned. 'Perhaps because I believed I'd soon get over it, forget you eventually or remember you as a passing fancy. But I couldn't get you out of my mind or my blood. Writing, other women, drink – none of them could blot out the memory of you and the times we'd had together. Do you believe me?'

'I want to – you've no idea how much I want to,' she whispered.

'Twelve months after we'd parted I was still missing you, so I sent you a copy of my first novel, hoping to break the deadlock between us. I hoped you'd reply and I'd find out what you were doing and how you were feeling. I hoped we'd meet again and I'd find out if the magic was still there.' He groaned again as her roving fingers touched a potent hidden nerve and he buried his lips against the curve of her throat, his teeth biting the thin skin. 'If you're going to do things like that to me you'll have to take the consequences,' he growled in a savage undertone, and before she could withdraw from him he swept her off her feet and carried her over to the bed.

Beneath them the antique velvet quilt, hand-stitched years ago by some creative housewife with a flair for colour and design, provided a rich and sumptuous couch for their moon-silvered bodies, its soft plush titillating their skins, and for a while they lay facing each other, kissing and caressing each other gently, indulging their senses until a turbulence swelled exquisitely in both of them, causing them to entwine more closely.

'I've missed you too,' sighed Karen, the words forced out at last past the barrier of her pride by the love which was springing up spontaneously in response to his confession. 'After I left you in London, I think a part of me died.'

'Why didn't you tell me you felt like that?' Val demanded, leaning up on one elbow to hover above her, his moonlight-reflecting eyes seeming to shoot sparks at her.

'I was afraid you'd have laughed at me and rejected me if I'd asked you to go with me or if I'd tried to tie you down. You see, I respected the promises we'd made to each other about no strings. That's why I didn't tell you about Tony.' Her breath quivered in her throat as she remembered the hours of unhappiness she had suffered when she had longed to get in touch with him but had suppressed the longing. 'I didn't want you to feel you had to marry me only because I was going to have your child. I didn't want you to feel I'd trapped you. And you would have felt trapped, wouldn't you?' she asked urgently, wanting to be told she had done the right thing; wanting to be reassured that her proud sacrifice of her own emotional needs and physical desires had not been in vain.

'Maybe,' he admitted, lying down again, but not close to her, lying on his back and not touching her any more, looking at the moon-bright window. 'Maybe you're right, I would have felt trapped,' he said slowly and thoughtfully.

'And if you'd felt trapped you'd have . . . well, sooner or later you'd have hated me, resented both me and the child, and you'd have left us.' She caught the bright flash of his eyes as he glanced sideways at her. 'And I don't think I could have borne that.' Her voice shook again. 'It was better to live apart from you, remembering the happiness we'd known together, remembering how . . . how much I'd loved you than to live with you and see you destroy our relationship with resentment and hate.'

There was a long silence and she sensed his thoughts had gone far away from her. Wanting to be close to him again, she laid her cheek against the cushion of his shoulder. Raising a hand, Val stroked her hair gently as if to comfort her. At last he said quietly,

'I've always hated you. Hating you has been a part of loving you.'

'Why?' She raised her head to stare at him in amazement. 'Why have you hated me?'

'For being the one woman I've ever known who has the power to hurt me, who's got beneath my skin and made me suffer. I hated you in London because I loved you so much I couldn't put an end to our affair when I thought it should have ended. I hated you after we parted because I couldn't forget you. I've hated you this past summer because you hadn't told me about Tony.' He turned to her abruptly, and the touch of his hands was hard and savage as he took hold of her head and glared down at her. 'Oh, yes, I've hated you more than you'll ever know, my sweet and only love.'

'Your only love?' she queried tauntingly, moving back from him, afraid suddenly of the violence which was in him. 'What about the other women in your life? What about Laurie?'

'Laurie?' His voice cracked with surprise. 'What about her?'

'She's kept house for you all summer. She's in love with you, and she told me herself you and she hit it off really well together. That was why she helped me to leave the island this afternoon. She didn't like me turning up out of your past. She wants to have you all to herself.'

Val's hands slid away from her head down to her throat.

'Well, this is news to me,' he drawled softly, one corner of his mouth quirking in an enigmatic smile. 'But let's not talk about Laurie now. She's not much more than a kid, in need of education in more ways than one, and why should I be interested in her when I have you here, with me on this bed, fascinating me with the mystery of your beautiful white body which has borne our son? It's you I want, Karen, you I need, not Laurie, so what are you going to do about it?'

It would be so easy to give in to the weakness which was flooding through her body again, to return to his arms and rekindle the fierce flame of passion in that moon-silvered room. Easy to give him what he wanted. Too easy.

'No, no, I can't—I can't,' she muttered, her hands against his bare chest as he came close to her again, pushing him away.

'What's wrong?' he whispered, and she felt his fingers lift lightly through her hair.

'I don't want it to happen,' she moaned.

'Why? Why fight something that's been inevitable from the time we met again in June?' he asked softly, his breath warm and seductive against her cheek. 'You and I always found it hard to stay out of each other's arms when we were in the same room. We're naturally attracted to each other. We can't help making love to each other. Karen,' his voice hardened and he withdrew from her so he could see her more clearly, 'you're not ashamed of what we did in London, are you? You're not ashamed of the way we loved?'

His nearness to her, the scents of his silky black hair and his moon-gilded skin were going to her head again. She had to get away from him before she gave in to that lovely, sensual weakness.

'Are you?' His voice grated harshly and his hands were on her arms now, hard and rough. 'Answer me, Karen, are you ashamed of having made love with me in the past?'

'No, no. I loved every minute of it ... but ... but if I make love with you now you mustn't think that anything has changed.'

'Anything?' His eyebrows slanted down towards the bridge of his nose and his eyes glittered with demoniacal fire again. 'What the hell do you mean by "anything"?'

'Please let go of me, Val. You're hurting my arms!' Karen protested, and he let go at once, his hands springing away from her arms as if he had been touched by a live wire. Seizing the opportunity of being temporarily free, Karen rolled away from him and off the bed. Wrapping her kimono about her, she tied the sash tightly at her waist. Away from him, she regained her coolness and let her head speak instead of her heart.

'I mean that, as I told you last night, I need more from a relationship with you or any other man than sexual gratification, and even if we did make love tonight it wouldn't change my mind. I would still go back to Canada tomorrow and take Tony with me.'

He lunged up on the bed, letting out one searing

expletive, obviously enraged by her remarks. Spinning on her heel, Karen wrenched open the door and fled from the room and along the landing to the other room where Tony was sleeping. She closed the door quickly and leaning against it waited with a wildly thumping heart for it to be forced open by Val, part of her hoping he would come, part of her hoping he wouldn't.

But he didn't come, and after a while she moved away from the door and taking off the kimono slipped into her nightgown, climbed into bed and swtched off the lamp. For a long time she lay with ears pricked, listening for any movement on the landing or for the opening of the door, trying to subdue the restless longings of her body.

She slept very little that night and wakened as soon as the sun rose. When she had dressed she opened the door of the bedroom cautiously, looked out, then went along the landing to pick up her toilet bag which was still lying on the floor opposite the open door of the other bedroom. As she bent down she glanced into the other bedroom. The bed was rumpled but empty. Val wasn't in the room.

Tony was a little grumpy when he was wakened because he hadn't really had enough sleep after his late night. Karen helped him to dress and then after repacking her overnight bag, went downstairs with him, holding his hand, determined not to let him out of her sight until they were both in the car and on their way to Seaton and Canada.

When she reached the attractive low-ceilinged entrance hall with its dark wooden beams, long oak refectory table and pretty Georgian windows Sue appeared in the doorway leading to the kitchen.

'Hi,' she said cheerfully. 'Ready for some break-fast? Just go into the first dining room and I'll bring it to you.'

The dining room was furnished with several square tables. Only one of them was covered with a flowered cloth and set with knives and forks. It was by one of the long windows which overlooked the land sloping away behind the back of the house.

'Where's Daddy?' demanded Tony as soon as he was sitting at the table.

'I don't know,' replied Karen truthfully, looking out of the window. It was another bright fall day. The sea glittered silvery blue, the sky was cloudless and amongst the long grasses the dried-up seeds of wild flowers glowed with reddish light in the sun-shine. Across the sea a distant mountain thrust a misty purple shoulder against the pale blue of the sky.

'Do you know where my daddy is?' Tony asked Sue when she came into the dining room carrying a tray on which there were two glasses of fruit juice, two bowls of cereal, a jug of milk and a pot of coffee.

'I sure do,' she replied as she set orange juice and cereal before him. 'He's gone to the island. He left just a few minutes ago with Titus in the truck. Now what would you like after the cereal? I have bacon and eggs and I can cook them any style you like.'

Karen ordered bacon and scrambled eggs for herself and a poached egg for Tony, and Sue left the room. Tony drank his juice and began to eat

his cereal. Karen sat stirring her coffee while she
looked out at the bright shimmer of the sunlight
on the sea.

So Val had gone back to the island, leaving her
free to go away with Tony, letting her leave him as
he had let her leave him in London. He hadn't
meant anything he had said last night—except perhaps the part about hating her. Now, after the
remark she had made about his lovemaking not
being enough to induce her to stay with him, he
had more cause to hate her. She had struck at his
pride in himself, and he would probably never for-
give her for implying that sexual gratification was
all he wanted from her.

Karen sighed wearily, leaning her head on her
hand. She felt so confused after the night of restless
longings and she was tired of trying to analyse her
own motives and Val's. Why not admit that she
could have enjoyed herself with him last night because for a while she had felt closer to him in spirit
than she had ever felt, because she had known for
a few glorious moments that they were made for
each other? So why had she run away from him?

It was that suspicion which kept swelling in her
mind every time Val kissed her or touched her that
he was deliberately using his knowledge of her response to his lovemaking to undermine her refusal
to marry him so that he could have Tony and
which crowded out all other feelings and thoughts;
an ugly, dangerous suspicion spawned by jealousy
and fear; jealousy of the life he had led without
her, of the other women, of Laurie; fear that once
he had obtained what he wanted from her, namely

Tony, he would leave her. That was why she had fled from his bed last night.

She became aware of a scraping sound, the noise of a chair being pushed across a bare wooden floor, and looked round. Tony was sliding down from his chair.

'Where are you going?' she asked.

'To look for Daddy.' He turned away from the table, but she grabbed his arm.

'Sit down, Tony. You haven't had all your breakfast yet.'

'No!' He tried to twist his arm free and failed because her hand had tightened around it. He glared at her with defiant grey eyes. 'You're hurting me!' he accused in the same way she had accused Val of hurting her when he had gripped her arms the previous might.

'Well, sit down, please,' she said more gently. 'Sue will be here with the rest of the breakfast in a minute.'

'I don't want any more breakfast. I want to go with Daddy to the island!' he cried, his voice rising querulously as he tried to pull free of her grasp. 'Let go of me!'

'Oh, please, Tony, sit down. We'll drive to Seaton to see if we can find him as soon as we've finished breakfast.'

'You promise?' he insisted, looking up at her with wary suspicious eyes; her own child suspicious of her! Karen could have wept.

'I promise,' she whispered.

To her relief he accepted her promise and climbed up on to his chair again. Sue came in with a tray and set down the plates of food.

'You must let me pay for Tony's and my bed and breakfast,' Karen said.

'Forget it,' replied Sue. 'Val is my cousin and you and Tony are his family, so I wouldn't think of accepting any payment from you.'

'But we're not Val's family.'

'Aren't you?' Sue's eyes were coldly mocking. 'Last night and this morning I got the impression that you are. Val loves both of you and he wants to take care of you in the same way that Titus loves and takes care of David, Benjy and me, so to my mind that means you and Tony are Val's family. And you would be married, would have been married years ago if you hadn't been so darned proud and independent. That's the trouble with clever women like you. Your minds are so cluttered up with notions about being free you don't understand love. Love is commitment, not freedom. It's giving, not taking.' Sue's mouth widened into a grin. 'And now I'm not going to *give* you a chance to reply, because I can hear Benjy yelling. It's time I bathed and fed him.'

When she and Tony had finished eating Karen took some dollar bills from her bag and laid them on the table as payment, then taking Tony by the hand she left the hotel. She was unlocking the door of the car when a red and cream pick-up truck trundled down the slope and stopped near her. Tall and lean in his overalls and checked shirt, Titus Allan got out of the truck and loped over to her.

'You just leavin'?' he drawled. 'Goin' to Seaton?'

'Yes,' she replied. 'Get in, Tony.' The little boy scrambled into the front passenger seat.

'Val's gone over to the island.' Titus glanced at his watch. 'Reckon he's there now. He said to tell you he'll be back at the wharf in Seaton about eleven o'clock and he'll see you there. Okay?'

'Oh, yes, yes, of course. Thank you.' Karen held out a hand to him. 'And thank you and Sue for your hospitality and all you did for us last night.'

'Think nothing of it,' he said, shaking her hand. 'See you around Karen. You too, Tony. When you're down this way again you and David will have to get together. So long now.'

Red maple and silver birches blazed crimson and gold against the dark blue-greens of pines and spruce in the woods that crowded down to the edge of the road and the black shadows of trees made a lacy pattern on the sunlit surface of the road. Tony sat up on the edge of the seat, looking out,

'What time is it?' he asked.

'Twenty after ten,' Karen replied, frowning a little as the car's engine gave a cough, seemed to stop, picked up again, coughed again and stopped completely. Coasting into the side of the road, she pushed the lever into park, braking the car. She turned the key in the ignition. The engine turned over but didn't start. On the dashboard a light gleamed like a baleful red eye, and peering at it she saw that it was warning her she was out of fuel. She glanced at the fuel gauge incredulously. The needle pointed to E for empty.

'What's wrong, Mummy?' asked Tony.

'The fuel tank is empty,' she groaned, and looked

around her. All she could see were trees, some dark, some bright, and the ribbon of the road curving away round a bend.

'What'll we do?' asked Tony, his voice trembling a little.

'I guess we'll have to walk back to the inn and ask Titus if he has any fuel he can lend us. Come on, get out.'

Tony slid off the seat on to the road and Karen shut the doors and locked them. Holding his hand, she started to walk back the way they had come, trying to guess how far the distance was. Fifteen minutes later, pulling Tony along behind her, she trudged down the slope to the inn and knocked on the front door.

Fortunately Titus did have a can of fuel which he carried for emergencies, and he drove Karen and Tony back to the parked car in his truck and poured the fuel into the tank for her.

'That should get you as far as the service station by the wharf in Seaton,' he said. 'Take care, now.'

'What time is it?' Tony asked again as soon as they were on the road.

'Nearly eleven,' Karen replied.

'Will Daddy wait for us?'

'I don't know,' she said, giving him a sidelong look. She hadn't realised he had heard what Titus had said about Val meeting them at the wharf at eleven o'clock. Before she had found out she had run out of fuel she had intended to drive right through Seaton towards Milworth and the road west to Bangor and places beyond. She had intended to go straight back to Canada. Now she would have to stop to pick up fuel near the wharf, and if Val was there waiting, Tony was bound to see him even if Val didn't see them.

Why had Val sent that message through Titus? Why had he gone back to the island only to return to Seaton? Arrogant to the last, he assumed that she would obey him and would be there to meet him. To do what? To return to the island with him? How could he possibly assume she would do that after what she had said to him in the bedroom that morning?

The road widened as the thick woods gave way to houses, some of them old, built in Colonial style with shutters edging their sash windows and spider-web fanlights curving over their doorways; some of them modern, long low sprawling ranch-type bungalows. The road dipped downwards to the edge of the shining bay. Ahead was the service station with its blue and red fuel pumps in front of its white garages.

Karen stopped the car beside one of the pumps, turned off the engine and sat staring straight ahead of her, pretending she couldn't see the tall man who was striding across the road from the wharf.

'There's Daddy!' exclaimed Tony excitedly, and was out of the car before she could do or say anything. Beside her the pump attendant looked in at the open car window.

'Can I help you, ma'am?' he asked.

'Fill it up, please,' she said, and opening the door got out to follow Tony.

'I was beginning to think you weren't coming or

that Titus hadn't given you my message,' drawled Val. He was dressed in the grey tweed jacket and dark slacks he had worn at the luncheon given in his honour at the inn in June, and in the sunlight his well-brushed hair shone like the plumage on a blackbird's wing. He was carrying a zipped valise in one hand and his other hand held a parka slung over one of his shoulders. Vigorous and determined, he stepped around her and walked towards the car, Tony hopping excitedly after him. When he reached the car Val said something to Tony, who disappeared round the door of the car which Karen had left open. In a few seconds Tony emerged, the car keys glinting in his little hand, and followed Val to the rear of the car.

Karen was spurred into action and marched over to them.

'What are you doing?' she demanded.

'Putting my luggage in the trunk,' Val replied calmly, slanting her a cool, mocking glance. 'Would you like me to drive for a while?'

He banged the trunk closed and turned to look at her. Immediately, so it seemed to her, the old familiar magic wreathed itself about her and her heart began to beat erratically. She tried to speak, but couldn't because her tongue seemed to be stuck to the roof of her mouth. She could only stare up at him as hope began to blossom within her.

'You seem to be at a loss for words, sweetheart,' Val whispered tauntingly, and bending his head kissed her briefly and provocatively on the mouth. 'I'm coming with you and Tony.'

'Why?' Her lips shaped the word, but no sound came from her dry throat.

'To prove to you once and for all that I also want more from our relationship than mere sexual gratification,' he replied with a wry twist to his mouth. 'I'm going to stay with you until you've climbed down from that high perch of pride which you're on at the moment and can accept my proposal of marriage.'

'Shall I check the oil, ma'am?' asked the pump attendant, looking at her over Val's shoulder and winking one eye at her mockingly.

'Yes, please,' she croaked.

She looked up at Val. The greenish grey eyes glinted back at her.

'We'll have a proper wedding,' he told her. 'Quiet but correct, and we'll invite your family and Sue and Titus and their kids because they're the only family I have, and we'll make before them all the proper promises, the ones we should have made years ago.'

'For . . . for Tony's sake?' Karen whispered, her suspicions dying hard.

'For Tony's sake, for the sake of our next child, but most of all for our sakes, for you and me, to make up for what we were cheated of seven years ago through our own foolish pride. I want to marry you because I want to keep you and support you, because I want to have the right to say you're my wife as well as my love. For the third time of asking, Karen, will you marry me?'

Her glance wavered from his to Tony's face, peeping at her from behind Val's hip. The grey eyes were shining up at her expectantly.

'Go on, Mummy,' Tony urged. 'Say yes! I'll run away if you don't!'

'Blackmailer!' she retorted shakily, and suddenly all her pride crumbled to dust and she surrendered, not to Val but to her love for him and for their child. 'I'll marry you,' she whispered, her arms reaching out and going round him, and there, standing in the bright sunlight with fallen leaves whispering about their feet, they kissed again passionately, pledging commitment to each other at last, watched in delight by the excited, jumping Tony, the grinning pump attendant and some passersby who had paused to stare.

They didn't hurry on the drive westwards along the road which wound across the wooded hills of Maine and through the Green Mountains of Vermont, because every moment spent together was suddenly very precious and had to be savoured to the full. Before them the coloured woods, red and bronze, gold and green, unfolded slowly in a sun-shot haze until at last, as the sun began to set in a sky streaked with crimson and gold cloud behind the dark mysterious pointed peaks of the distant Adirondack Mountains, they came to the glimmering sky-reflecting waters of the long lake which divides Vermont from the State of New York and is named after the great French explorer Samuel Champlain.

They crossed the lake by ferryboat and drove to an old stone lodge which had been converted into a hotel. There, after Tony had gone to bed, they ate by candlelight, looking out at the moon-dazzled waters of the lake, and later they slept together in the centre of a wide king-sized bed.

Next morning when she woke up Karen lay in drowsy contentment, watching the sky change from dark blue to pearly grey, and wondered at the change in herself, amazed that commitment could bring such a feeling of ease and well-being.

'It's a new beginning, a clean and empty page, a fresh start,' she murmured aloud.

'What is?' Val's voice was slurred with sleepiness.

'This is,' she replied. 'You and I having another chance to live together.' She turned to him, suddenly doubtful, not of him this time, but of herself and her own ability to make him happy and keep him with her. 'Oh, I hope I don't make any mistakes this time,' she whispered. 'I hope I don't smudge the page.' She buried her face against his chest, drawing strength from his warmth, holding him tightly as if she were afraid he might leave her, there and then.

'You'll make mistakes and so will I,' he murmured, winding a hand in her hair and pulling her head back so he could see her face. 'But as long as you don't make the same mistake you did before, as long as you don't make the mistake of believing I don't love you, our marriage will survive.' He touched her cheek with gentle fingers and his smiling lips brushed her temple in a light kiss. 'Would you like to tell me how you made that mistake?' he asked softly.

'The day I had to go home to Canada you let me go,' she replied. 'You didn't try to stop me from going, or offer to go with me. Nor did you follow me. Then you didn't write to me, so I assumed you didn't love me.'

'And that was my mistake too. I believed you didn't love me, that you wanted to be free, so I thought I could let you go.' His arm tightened about her waist, his eyes blazed with green fire and his mouth took on a taut arrogant curve. 'I'll never make that mistake again. That's why I'm here, why I'm going with you. Now I've found you again I'm damned if I'm going through another seven years of deprivation. To hell with pride and to hell with being free! I'm going to tie you to me with as many strings as I can find, so many it will take you years to undo the knots, and as fast as you undo one I'll tie another.'

'And I'll help you to tie them,' Karen cried happily as she willingly surrendered at last to love's dominion.

The communicating door between their room and the next one burst open suddenly and a small energetic boy in flannel pyjamas raced across the room and flung himself across the bottom of the bed. Finding a way under the bedclothes, he began to burrow his way between them until his head, covered with tousled black hair, popped up close to theirs.

'Hi, you two,' said Tony, grinning at them, his eyes shining. 'Now that I've got a real daddy, Mummy, do you think I could have a little baby brother or sister?'

Above the child's dark head Karen's eyes met Val's in a glance of shared love and laughter.

'I think that could be arranged,' she said, ruffling Tony's hair affectionately.

'But not until after we're married,' whispered Val, his hand covering hers where it rested on Tony's head.

'No, not until after we're married,' she agreed wholeheartedly.

Four weeks later, wearing a demure blue silk dress with frills at its high neckline and at the edge of its hem, and carrying a small posy of white rosebuds, Karen walked down the aisle of the church which she had attended most of her life with her parents and sister. Beside her walked Bill Mather, her brother-in-law, who had consented to give her away. Behind them walked Iris, as maid of honour, and Tony as pageboy.

At the chancel steps a tall man with thick black hair stood waiting. He was dressed in a neat dark suit and as she approached him he turned to smile at her, his greenish-grey eyes ablaze with the intensity of his feelings. Karen took her place beside him and together they listened to and then repeated the elegant yet simple words of the promises which have been made and are still being made by millions of couples; the promises to love and to cherish, in sickness and in health.

And as they kissed to seal their vows Karen whispered,

'Better late than never.'

'Better *now* than never,' Val retorted softly, and

together they turned to kneel before the priest to receive his blessing and his words of wisdom and advice.

Harlequin® |Plus|

A WORD ABOUT THE AUTHOR

Born in the port of Liverpool, England, Flora Kidd grew up to love the sea. She spent many hours with her father strolling the banks of the River Mersey, watching ships bring cargo from magic-sounding places.

While she attended university, her interest in sailing brought Flora into contact with her husband-to-be, Wilf, also a sailing enthusiast. After their marriage, he worked as a design engineer and she taught in a girls' school; from their combined earnings they saved ... not for a home but for a sailing dinghy!

Eventually they moved to Scotland, where they lived in an old stone house on the Ayrshire coast. In those peaceful mountainous surroundings, with the Firth of Clyde in view, Flora began to think seriously about writing—and it wasn't long before her first novel, *Nurse at Rowanbank* (#1058), was accepted for publication.

Today the author and her family make their home in New Brunswick, one of Canada's Atlantic provinces. The Bay of Fundy has now joined the River Mersey and the Firth of Clyde as yet another maritime setting for Flora Kidd's delightful love stories.

ANTIGUA KISS
ANNE WEALE

The exciting new bestseller by one of the world's top romance authors!

Christie's marriage to Caribbean playboy
Ash Lombard was to be for convenience only.
He promised never to touch her. That was fine
by Christie, a young widow whose unhappy first
marriage had destroyed the passionate side of
her nature—but it wasn't long before she
learned Ash had no intention of
keeping his word....

Available in January wherever paperback books are sold, **or** send your
name, address and zip or postal
code, along with a check or
money order for $3.70
(includes 75¢ for
postage and handling)
payable to Harlequin
Reader Service, to:

**Harlequin
Reader Service**

In the U.S.:
P.O. Box 22188
Tempe, AZ 85282

In Canada:
649 Ontario Street
Stratford, Ontario
N5A 6W2

HELP HARLEQUIN PICK 1982's GREATEST ROMANCE!

We're taking a poll to find the most romantic couple (real, not fictional) of 1982. Vote for any one you like, but please vote and mail in your ballot today. As Harlequin readers, you're the real romance experts!

Here's a list of suggestions to get you started. Circle your choice, <u>or</u> print the names of the couple you think is the most romantic in the space below.

Prince of Wales / Princess of Wales

Luke / Laura (General Hospital stars)

Gilda Radner / Gene Wilder

Jacqueline Bisset / Alexander Godunov

Mark Harmon / Christina Raines

Carly Simon / Al Corley

Susan Seaforth / Bill Hayes

Burt Bacharach / Carole Bayer Sager

_____
(please print)
_____
_____

Please mail to: Maureen Campbell
Harlequin Books
225 Duncan Mill Road
Don Mills, Ontario, Canada
M3B 3K9

POLL-1